# "It's only one night, after all."

Their eyes locked and his widened slightly.

And then he knew. Knew what she was saying. She would give him one night. And give *herself* one night. With him.

She watched him struggle with what she knew had to be a compellingly wicked temptation.

"It's your decision," he said slowly, but his fists remained balled up by his side.

"I've already made up my mind," she said.

"So be it," he said, and as he stared deep into her eyes his own were strangely cold, yet full of a dark triumph.

**MIRANDA LEE** is Australian, living near Sydney. Born and raised in the bush, she was boarding-school educated and briefly pursued a classical music career before moving to Sydney and embracing the world of computers. Happily married, with three daughters, she began writing when family commitments kept her at home. She likes to create stories that are believable, modern, fast-paced and sexy. Her interests include reading meaty sagas, doing word puzzles and going to the movies.

# Miranda Lee

## JUST FOR A NIGHT

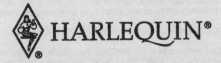

TORONTO • NEW YORK • LONDON
AMSTERDAM • PARIS • SYDNEY • HAMBURG
STOCKHOLM • ATHENS • TOKYO • MILAN • MADRID
PRAGUE • WARSAW • BUDAPEST • AUCKLAND

ISBN 0-373-12164-4

JUST FOR A NIGHT

First North American Publication 2001.

Visit us at www.eHarlequin.com

Printed in U.S.A.

# CHAPTER ONE

'I DON'T want you to go.'

Marina looked up from her suitcase and shook her head at the sulky expression on her fiancé's face.

'Please don't start that again, Shane. I *have* to go. Surely you can see that?'

'No, I can't,' he snapped. 'It's only three weeks till the wedding and here you are swanning off to the other side of the world on some wild-goose chase. There's no guarantee that your bone marrow will save that little girl's life. You're probably just getting their hopes up for nothing.'

'Firstly, I will only be away a week at the most,' Marina pointed out, impatience only a breath away. 'Secondly, I happen to be a near perfect match. Not only in blood, but in tissue type. Do you know how rare that is?'

'I'm sure you'll tell me,' he said sourly. 'You're the smart one around here.'

Marina frowned at his tone of voice, and at the indication behind his words. This was a side to Shane she'd never seen before.

There again, she considered slowly, she'd never crossed him before. After her mother's death a couple of months ago she'd been more than happy to accept the warm hand of friendship and support Shane had offered, more than happy to have someone there to make all the funeral arrangements and give her a shoulder to cry on. Her usually decisive and strong-willed character had failed her entirely during that grief-stricken time. Shane had been strong when she'd felt weak, kind and thoughtful when that was what she'd needed most.

That his kindness had ended up in his bed had probably been inevitable. He was an attractive man and she was, after all, so terribly lonely. Her satisfaction with his lovemaking had not been quite so inevitable, given her uninspiring sexual history. The pleasure he'd given her had stunned her, so much so that she'd believed herself in love at last. When he'd asked her to marry him a month ago, she'd said yes.

Now she stared at him. His face was not so handsome as he scowled at her. His eyes not so kind, either. They were cold and angry.

'I had no idea how much you resented my being a teacher,' she said, covering her distress behind a cool tone. 'If you imagine I think you're in any way inferior to me because you work with your hands, then I don't.'

Shane had been her mother's right-hand man in the riding and dressage school she'd run on the outskirts of Sydney. Although a high school drop-out, Shane was far from dumb. When Marina's mother had hired him a good few years back, the then twenty-five-year-old had known everything there was to know about matters equestrian. He'd got along with Marina's mother like a house on fire because they had a passion in common: the passion for horses.

Marina quite liked horses, and she'd learnt to ride adequately enough, but she'd never been obsessed by the showjumping scene, as her mother and Shane were. She'd always quite liked Shane too, but he'd been standoffish in her presence—till her mother's illness and death had changed the status quo between them.

After they'd become engaged, Marina had told Shane that the school and the horses were his to do with whatever he liked.

She wondered now if he loved the school and horses more than he loved her.

Or if he loved her at all...

'Maybe our getting married is not such a good idea,' she said quietly. 'We did rush into it a bit.'

He was around the bed and taking her in his arms before she could say boo. But his hard, hungry kisses left her cold. Shane stopped after a while and held her at arm's length. This time his expression was full of apology and remorse.

'You're angry with me,' he said. 'And you've every right to be. I was being bloody selfish. Of course you have to go. Of course. It's just that I'm going to miss you terribly, sweetheart.' He released her arms to cup her chin and lift her mouth for him to kiss again. Softly this time. And sweetly.

Marina had to admit to a moment of melting. These new sexual responses of hers could be very disarming.

And perhaps not always in her best interests, came the astonishing realisation.

'I'm really going to miss this beautiful mouth of yours,' Shane murmured. 'There again, everything about you is so beautiful. Your eyes. Your skin. Your hair. Your breasts.' His hands lifted to stroke them through her shirt and she was dismayed at the way they responded, as though they weren't connected with her brain.

'I've always wanted you, Marina,' he insisted, with a thickened quality to his voice. 'From the first moment I saw you. But your mother warned me right from the start that I could look, but not touch. Her little princess was not for the likes of me.'

Marina was not really surprised by this news. Her mother had been a very contradictory person. British-born and bred, she'd apparently defied her wealthy, upper-crust parents to run off to Australia with a colonial stablehand. She'd been told never to darken their doorstep again. Which she hadn't.

Her bitterness over their attitude had been such that she'd never spoken of her English ancestors to her daughter, and had forbidden Marina to ever seek them out.

One would have thought she'd bring up Marina to despise this kind of snobbery and hypocrisy. And she had, in a way. But at the same time, perversely, she'd tried to turn her only daughter into a right little madam, with all the associated refinements and manners. Marina had been given ballet lessons, piano lessons and speech and drama lessons, not to mention the obligatory riding and dressage lessons.

It hadn't really worked. Marina might look an elegant twenty-five-year-old lady on the surface, and she could hold her own in any company, but she was still Australian through and through—with a stubborn streak a mile long, an instinctive irreverence for authority and a pragmatic no-nonsense attitude to life.

She was also a chip off the old block when it came to defying parents, because when she'd gone to England on a backpacking holiday a couple of years previously she had tried to look up the maternal side of her family—her mother's maiden name being on her birth certificate—only to find that there were more Binghams in England than you could poke a stick at.

Without more information to narrow the field, or money to hire an investigator, finding the right Binghams would have been like looking for a needle in a haystack. Since she had never been all *that* curious about the English side to her family—they sounded horrible snobs to her—she'd given up the search without another qualm.

Shane's comment reminded her that she would be in England again soon. And this time she *did* have some money. Her mother's estate had been larger than she'd envisaged. It seemed she'd been a very astute businesswoman over the years. Now that Marina could not hurt her mother with a more in-depth search, she might just see if she could find her grandparents, plus any possible aunts, uncles and cousins.

And maybe she wouldn't.

They'd never searched for her, had they? Why should she care a whit for them? They'd probably only upset her by not wanting to have anything to do with her.

No, she would abandon that idea entirely. Best to let sleeping dogs lie.

'I never thought you'd look twice at me,' Shane was saying, 'with your private school education and your looks. But you did, didn't you, princess? And now...now you're mine.' He bent to back his claim with a long and very intimate kiss. It did set her heart a-thudding, but it was not what she wanted at that moment. All she wanted was to be left alone. Her head was absolutely whirling.

'Come back as quickly as you can,' he urged. 'Don't stay over there a moment longer than necessary.'

Marina didn't know what to say. She felt very confused. A couple of weeks ago she had not been able to wait to marry Shane. Now, suddenly, those heady feelings of being madly in love seemed to have disappeared and her thoughts were very disturbing.

Surely Shane could not be just marrying her for the horses. Surely he loved her. And surely she loved him back. Hadn't she quivered under his touch only last night? Hadn't she cried out with pleasure?

Her mental toing and froing led nowhere, but the urge to get away from Shane remained acute. The urge to get away all round was becoming even stronger.

The trip to London, which had loomed in her mind

as something of a trial, now took on a different perspective. It became a welcome escape, a time away from Shane during which she could think more clearly. By the time she returned, hopefully, she would know what to do.

It would not be too late to break her engagement even then. It wasn't as though they were going to have a big church wedding, only a simple ceremony in her mother's prized rose garden, with a celebrant and a few close friends attending.

This had been Shane's wish, not Marina's. She'd always wanted a traditional wedding, but Shane had argued the unsuitability of a big celebration so soon after her mother's death. She recalled Shane had also said it would be a waste of money—money better spent on the plans he had for building new stables and buying new horses.

Money figured a lot in Shane's arguments, Marina was beginning to realise.

When the phone call had come from the children's hospital, asking her if she could fly to London as soon as possible to be a bone marrow donor, Shane's first concern had been how much money it would cost and who was going to pay. He hadn't shut up about it till a follow-up letter had arrived, explaining Marina would not be out of pocket in any way whatsoever.

Shane *still* hadn't been happy about her going.

But in this case Marina had remained adamant, her natural tendency to stubbornness rising up through the uncharacteristic submissiveness which had been plaguing her. This had nothing to do with them as a couple and everything to do with herself as a decent and caring human being. She was prepared to go even if she had to pay for it all herself. How could she not, when a little girl's life was at stake?

Her name was Rebecca, and she was only seven. An orphan, God love her, but with a wonderful great-uncle, it seemed. An earl, no less. And rich as Croesus, thank heavens.

He'd sent a first-class return ticket for Marina, plus a written assurance that he would be personally responsible for all her expenses. His gratitude knew no bounds. He claimed he would be in her debt for the rest of his life.

Marina smiled as she thought of the letter and its incredibly formal-sounding expressions. The man was British aristocracy through and through, all right. But rather sweet, she conceded. For a blue-blood.

'Ahh, you're smiling,' Shane said, and bent to peck her on the lips. 'I must be forgiven.'

Marina could not trust herself to speak. She twisted out of Shane's arms and busied herself shutting and locking her suitcase. 'We'll have to leave for the airport shortly,' she said. 'If you're still going to drive me, that is?'

'Why wouldn't I drive you?' he said expansively. 'Don't be so sensitive, sweetheart.' He scooped the suitcase off the bed and placed his spare arm around her shoulders.

'I know why you're so touchy,' he said, hugging her to his side. 'You're just jumpy about the flight. And about your hospital stay at the other end. I'll say this for you, Marina, you're damned brave, volunteering to have needles poked in you like that. I know I wouldn't do it. Not for a perfect stranger.'

Marina frowned. She didn't think of herself as particularly brave. She'd been assured the procedure was not painful, though there might be some discomfort in her hip for a couple of days.

It dawned on her then that Shane was a very selfish man. Selfish and ambitious and stingy.

Marina fingered her engagement ring all the way from Bringelly to the airport at Mascot. Half a dozen times she contemplated taking it off and giving it back. But she didn't. And, in the end, she boarded the plane still an engaged woman.

## CHAPTER TWO

THE man holding the sign which said 'MISS MARINA SPENCER' didn't look like a chauffeur.

He wasn't wearing a uniform for one thing, like several of the other sign-carrying chauffeurs standing near him. He was wearing a black pin-striped three-piece suit and a crisp white business shirt whose starched collar was neatly bisected by a classy maroon tie. A matching maroon handkerchief winked from the breast pocket of the superbly tailored jacket.

Frankly, he looked like an executive. A very tall, very good-looking, very successful executive. In his early thirties, Marina guessed, he had straight black hair—impeccably parted and groomed—straight black brows, and an air of urbane superiority. She could see him sitting behind a desk, in one of those black leather swivel chairs. Or in a boardroom, at the head of one of those long, polished tables.

But the sign he was carrying placed him very firmly as the chauffeur she'd been told would meet her at Heathrow. So Marina set her luggage trolley on an unswerving path straight towards him.

His gaze, which had been staring rather blankly at the steady stream of arrivals, shifted abruptly to hers, and Marina found herself looking into deeply set blue eyes which widened at her approach. Clearly she didn't fit his idea of a Miss Marina Spencer any more than *he* did her concept of a chauffeur.

Admittedly, she probably didn't look like most Englishmen's idea of a girl from Sydney. Her bright red hair and very pale skin did not fit the clichéd beach beauties from Bondi, sporting honey-blonde hair as long as their legs and a gorgeous all-over tan.

At least I have the long legs, she thought, smiling ruefully to herself over her total inability to tan—inherited, possibly, from somewhere on her maternal side. Unless it came from her father's distant Irish ancestry. Who knew, where recessive genes were concerned? Luckily, Marina's mother had lathered her daughter's sensitive skin with sun factor fifteen her entire life, and she only carried a smattering of light freckles.

Marina stopped the trolley right in front of the chauffeur and smiled politely up into his by now frowning face.

'I'm Marina Spencer,' she informed him.

He gave her the longest look in return, one which left her feeling as poorly composed as the twenty-two-hour flight had. She'd hardly slept a wink, for one thing. And something she'd eaten had not agreed with her. All in all, the trip *had* been a trial, and she wasn't looking forward to the return flight, regardless of the first-class seat.

She'd done her best to resurrect her appearance in the Ladies just before disembarking, but despite fresh make-up her skin still felt dehydrated, and her normally vibrant red-gold curls hung rather limply around her face and shoulders. Her widely spaced green eyes, one of her best features, had dark smudges under them.

On the plus side, her jeans had survived the trip better than a skirt or a dress. And her favourite and thankfully crease-proof black jacket hid the wrinkles in the white shirt underneath.

But she still felt somewhat the worse for wear.

The chauffeur's thorough visual assessment irritated her somewhat. Finally, he bent to prop the sign against a nearby pillar, then straightened, still unsmiling, to hold out his hand to her in greeting.

'How do you do, Miss Spencer? I trust you had a good flight? I'm James Marsden.' The fingers which enclosed hers were firm and cool. 'My chauffeur had a problem with one of his knees this morning. Arthritis. So I came to collect you myself. He's waiting for us out in the car.'

Marina blinked her astonishment. *This* was James Marsden? *This* was Rebecca's great-uncle? *This* was the Earl of Winterborne?

Her first impulse was to laugh. No wonder he hadn't fitted the image of a chauffeur. But, my goodness, he didn't fit her image of the Earl of Winterborne, either. She'd pictured an elderly white-haired gentleman, with a handle-bar moustache, a walking stick and an Irish wolfhound at his feet.

'That was very kind of you,' she said, trying to school her mouth into a polite expression instead of an amused grin. She succeeded, but not before the Earl of Winterborne clearly spotted her struggle to suppress a smile. Those straight black brows of his drew momentarily together, and for a brief second she thought he was going to ask her what the joke was. But he merely shrugged and stepped forward to lift her suitcase from the trolley, swinging it easily to the ground at his feet.

'Is this your only luggage?' he asked.

'Yes, it is.' She was glad now that she'd brought only her best clothes with her. Glad too that she'd had a new suitcase to pack them in. The bag she'd brought to England on her previous visit would have proved a right embarrassment.

This one was an elegant tapestry model in smoky blues and greys which she'd bought from one of the chain stores during the after-Christmas sales at the beginning of the year. It had a roomy matching shoulder bag which was at that moment hanging fairly heavily on one of her slender shoulders, filled to the brim with everything she'd thought she might need on the long flight over.

'You travel light, Miss Spencer.'

She almost laughed again. He wasn't carrying her leaden shoulder bag. She smiled instead. 'Do call me Marina. Please.'

Now *he* smiled, if you could call a slight upward movement at one corner of his nicely shaped lips a smile. 'Australians have a penchant for using first names quickly, don't they?'

'We don't stand on ceremony, I guess,' she agreed, and wondered if she had offended him in some way.

There was a dryness to his voice which could have been sarcasm. Or disapproval.

The demi-smile disappeared as quickly as it had come. He was as stiffly formal in life as he'd been in his letters, she decided. But where his written words had seemed rather sweet, his blue-blood bearing and autocratic manner were not so endearing. Frankly, they were intimidating. Marina determined not to succumb to the temptation to kowtow and grovel, reminding herself he was just a flesh and blood man underneath the cloak of superiority he wore so arrogantly, yet so very elegantly.

'So what should *I* call *you*?' she asked. 'What does an earl get called, anyway?'

There was a minute lifting of his eyebrows, as though her casual attitude was to be expected but only just tolerated. 'My Lord, usually,' came his cool reply. 'Or Lord Winterborne, in my case.'

His pompousness sparked a touch of rebellion. 'That sounds awfully stiff. How can you stand it? At home you'd simply be called James. Or Jim. Or even Jack. Still, when in Rome do as the Romans do, I guess. I wouldn't want to do anything which wasn't appropriate while I'm over here.'

He gave her another of those highly disturbing looks. 'No, of course not,' he drawled, and his eyes dropped to her left hand and her diamond engagement ring.

Marina could not believe the thought which flashed into her mind. Immediately prickles of heat whooshed into her cheeks. When his eyes lifted back to her face, she hoped and prayed he could not read the reason behind her most uncustomary blush.

'Then call me James, by all means,' he said with starch-filled gallantry. 'Come.' He lifted her suitcase from the floor beside him with his right hand while he put his left at her elbow. 'You must be tired. I will take you to my apartment in Mayfair where you can have some decent food and a rest. Then, this afternoon, I will take you to the hospital to meet Rebecca.'

Marina felt guilty that she'd forgotten her mission for a moment. 'How *is* Rebecca?' she asked anxiously. This is what you've come for, she lectured herself sternly. Not to have unconscionable thoughts about the Earl of Winterborne.

'She's very much looking forward to meeting you,' he replied. 'I must warn you, though, she's very thin and she's lost all of her hair through the chemotherapy. So try not to look shocked when you walk in. Rebecca might only be seven but she's very much a girl, and very sensitive to her appearance.'

Marina's heart turned over. 'Oh, the poor little love,' she murmured.

The Earl of Winterborne gave a very un-earl-like sigh. It carried a weariness born of worry and grief, plus a type of resignation which came from feeling totally helpless. Marina understood perfectly what he was going through, because that was how she had felt while her mother had been dying of cancer. It was the reason why Marina had put herself on the bone marrow register. Because she'd wanted to give someone

else hope where there had been none for her mother—
or herself.

'Yes. Yes, that sums Rebecca up entirely,' he
agreed. His face had grown as bleak as his voice, and
his hand dropped away from Marina's elbow. The
suitcase was lowered to the floor once more. 'She's
had little enough love in her life so far. And little
enough luck. But that's been the way with things at
Winterborne Hall for quite some time.'

Marina found herself reaching out to put a com-
forting hand on his nearest sleeve. His handsome head
dipped slowly to glance down, first at her hand on his
arm and then up into her sympathetic gaze.

'Let's hope my coming will turn the tables, then,
shall we?' she said softly, giving his arm a gentle
squeeze before letting it fall back to her side.

He stared at her in silence for ages. Or so it seemed.
It was probably only a few seconds.

A thousand emotions seemed to flitter across his
face, none staying long enough for her to gauge properly. But she was left with the impression of a deep
distress, one which was disturbing him greatly.

'I would like to think so,' he said staunchly at long
last. 'But I have a feeling that might not be the case.
They say things are sent to try us,' he added in a
strangely bitter tone. 'To test our characters. I can see
that the next few days are going to test mine to the
limit.'

Marina was not sure what he meant. Had the doctors already given up all real hope for the child? Was
her own trip over here a waste of time, as Shane had

suggested? She wondered what other misfortunes had befallen his family lately. Marina suspected he had more on his mind than the health of the child. The Earl of Winterborne clearly had many burdens on his shoulders.

But they were very broad shoulders, she noted when he bent to pick up her suitcase a third time and began to stride off with it. She wondered if they would look as good without the suit. If they were mostly padding or real.

Marina frowned as she trotted after him. This was the second time in as many minutes that her mind had swung unexpectedly to the physical where this man was concerned. It wasn't like her to have thoughts such as this. Well, not till recently, anyway, and certainly not about any man other than Shane.

Not that she'd had anything to do with any man other than Shane lately. She'd taken compassionate leave from her teaching position after her mother's death and had stayed at home ever since, helping Shane with the administrative side of running the riding school. For the last few weeks her life had revolved around her fiancé and the astonishing things he could make her feel.

Her frown deepened as she tried to make sense of her unbidden responses to the Earl of Winterborne. Was her recent sexual awakening able to be transferred to any attractive man who came along? Had she turned into an ogler of male flesh? A female fantasiser?

The prospect appalled her. She'd never liked the

way some women talked about men and sex all the time when they were together, as though there was nothing else in their lives. Or the way they stared openly at certain parts of the male anatomy.

Marina's eyes drifted down from those broad shoulders to where Lord Winterborne's suit jacket outlined what looked like a nicely shaped *derrière*.

*You're doing it now,* that annoyingly honest voice piped in her head—the one which Marina could never deny.

*And enjoying it,* another sarcastic voice inserted slyly.

The first voice came to the rescue with a vengeance.

*And what's wrong with looking?* it challenged belligerently. *There's no harm in looking!*

*She wants to do more than look. She'd like to touch, too. She'd like to see if an English earl makes love like an Aussie stablehand. She'd like to—*

'Oh, do shut up!' she muttered aloud.

'Pardon?' The object of her mental warring glanced over his shoulder, slowing his stride at the same time.

Marina almost cannoned right into him. She stopped herself just in time, rocking backwards and forwards on her toes as she hitched the tapestry bag higher on her shoulder for added balance.

'Nothing,' she said with a blithe and decidedly false innocence. There was definitely nothing innocent going on in her mind at that moment. 'Just talking to myself.'

'You do that often?' His drily amused smile did

wickedly attractive things to his mouth. Marina decided she preferred him dead serious.

'All the time,' she admitted, wrenching her mind back from the path to hell with great difficulty. 'I was an only child, and only children often talk to themselves. I used to talk to a tea-towel as well.'

'A *tea-towel*?' He laughed, and Marina gritted her teeth. Laughing did to his whole face what that smile had done to his mouth: transformed it from merely handsome to lethally sexy.

'Why a tea-towel? Why not a doll? Or a teddy?'

Marina pulled a face. 'It's difficult to explain. The tea-towel wasn't another person, or a pretend friend. It was me. Or another side of me. My...secret side.'

'Sounds fascinating. Do you still talk to tea-towels?' he asked as he walked on, more slowly this time, so that she fell into step with him by his side.

'Not since I was eighteen.'

'What happened to you at eighteen?'

'I left home to go to teacher's college. I didn't think my new flatmates would indulge my peculiarities like my mother did. Since then, any conversations with my secret side take place in my head.'

He slanted a thoughtful glance across at her. 'And how often do these conversations take place?'

'Not that often nowadays.' But she had an awful feeling they were about to pick up frequency.

'Do you tell anyone about them?'

'Lord, no!'

'Not even your fiancé?'

Marina hesitated a fraction.

'That *is* an engagement ring on your finger, isn't it?'

'Yes.' Marina had pretty well decided on the flight over that she'd blown the incident before leaving home way out of proportion, that of course she loved Shane and wanted to marry him. But her responses to the man standing before her had shaken that conviction anew. How could she possibly be in love with Shane and feel attracted to the earl of Winterborne?

*It's possible because this is not love,* pointed out her pragmatic side. *It's just...attraction. He's a very attractive man.*

Marina found comfort in that thought. Yes, of course. Any woman would find this man attractive. He was the stuff female fantasies were made of. Handsome. Rich. Enigmatic. I'm not being disloyal to my feelings for Shane. I'm just being normal.

'No,' she answered levelly, after scooping in and letting out a steadying breath. 'I definitely don't tell Shane about them. He thinks I'm a very sensible, level-headed girl.'

That disturbing demi-smile surfaced again. 'And you're not?'

'I do try to be.' But I don't always succeed, she thought ruefully.

'When is your wedding?'

'In three weeks.'

'Three weeks!' He sounded shocked. And almost disbelieving. 'You've come all this way...and your wedding is only three weeks away?'

'I would have come,' she said truthfully, 'even if

the wedding had been tomorrow. My mother died of cancer. I could not have lived with myself if I had not come. And now that I have…I can't tell you how much I'm looking forward to doing this for your Rebecca. As soon as it can be arranged, actually. Tomorrow if you like. You did say the sooner the better in your letter, didn't you?'

He stopped and stared at her, then began shaking his head. 'You are one special lady, Miss Marina Spencer. One *very* special lady. Tomorrow would be marvellous. But I thought you'd be too tired.'

'What's tired in the scheme of things? I can rest afterwards.'

'And you will, too. As soon as you can leave the hospital, I'll take you down to Winterborne Hall, where you can relax for a few days before flying home. It's out in the country and quite beautiful at this time of year.'

'But…' A host of terrible thoughts rushed into her head which had nothing to do with relaxing. Marina tried to think of these new fantasies as just normal, but their explicit nature was very perturbing. 'No, I'm sorry. I really can't accept. For one thing I should be getting home to Shane. Besides, I… I wouldn't like to impose on Lady Winterborne like that.'

He simply *had* to have a wife, a man such as this. Please God, let him have a wife, Marina prayed. I would never think thoughts like this about a married man. I know I wouldn't.

'There *is* no Lady Winterborne,' he informed her coolly, and something inside her fluttered uncontrollably. 'But there are a dozen guest bedrooms just dying to be used. And plenty of staff to see to your every whim. What's a few days?' he added temptingly, his eyes searching hers. 'Your fiancé surely won't expect you to jump on a plane straight out of hospital?'

'I…I guess not. But I wouldn't like to put you to—'

'I insist,' he broke in brusquely. 'I will not take no for an answer.'

Marina swallowed. It was the wrong thing for him to say to her at that moment in time.

An image filled her mind, of her lying on a magnificent four-poster bed in one of those undoubtedly huge and plushly elegant guest bedrooms…

It was night, but there were candles casting an intimate glow through the room. Her red hair was spread out against a mountain of pillows, gleaming gold against pristine white. Her nightgown was virginal white as well, but made of satin and lace, and it hid little. She was reading when he came into the room, dressed in a rich purple robe. His penetrating blue eyes clashed with her own startled green ones. He walked arrogantly to the edge of the bed and shrugged out of the robe. He was naked. He climbed onto the bed and pulled the curtains so the world was shut out and darkness enveloped them. The book was taken from her suddenly trembling fingers. She felt a hand sliding around her neck, and her mouth being slowly lifted.

'I will not take no for an answer,' he whispered against her lips…

Marina's glazed eyes slowly cleared to find the

main star of her shockingly life-like fantasy staring at her with unconcealed concern.

'What is it? Are you not feeling well?'

Marina felt decidedly shaky, for such was the power of her imaginings.

'I...I *was* feeling a little faint there for a moment. But I'm all right now.' She scooped in a deep breath and did her best to still her wildly hammering heart.

'You had me worried. I thought I might have to carry *you* as well as the suitcase.'

For a split second Marina contemplated organising a faint.

'Do you think you can make it outside?' he asked, worry on his handsome face. 'It's not far.'

'Yes, of course,' she said briskly, disgusted with herself for this ongoing and quite uncharacteristic weakness. She had to get a hold of herself and her head once and for all. This would just not do!

'Lead on, My Lord,' she said firmly. 'I'll follow.'

He frowned. 'I thought you were going to call me James.'

'I know, but somehow it doesn't feel right.'

He looked slightly annoyed. 'Surely I'm not that intimidating?'

'Well, actually, yes, you are, Lord Winterborne.'

In more ways than one.

'But I would *prefer* you to call me James.'

'Sorry, Your Lordship. No can do.' This unfortunate attraction might be one-sided, but Marina still felt it only sensible to keep him at a distance. Calling him James was just too intimate for her peace of mind.

His glare fell just short of scowl. 'You really have a mind of your own, don't you?'

'Well, why not?' she said in a challenging tone. 'Don't English women?'

He laughed, but didn't answer her, she noted. After one last shake of his head, he stalked on ahead with her suitcase, leaving her to follow as she'd said she would.

# CHAPTER THREE

IT WAS raining outside—a light drizzle more like a mist than real rain. And it was freezing, by Marina's standards. After all, it was supposedly summer over here, unlike the actually warmer winter she'd left behind in Sydney. Of course it was still very early in the morning. Just going on six. The plane had landed in the dark, not long after five.

Still…

Marina thought of the clothes she'd brought and wondered if they'd do.

'Don't worry,' Lord Winterborne said when she glanced up at the sky. 'We have good heating inside. August can be like this. Very unpredictable. It will probably be fine and warm tomorrow. Ahh, here's William with the car.'

A large and stately-looking dark green saloon pulled into the kerb with a properly uniformed chauffeur behind the wheel. He looked about fifty, with a full, florid face and a few too many pounds around his stomach.

'Don't get out, William,' his employer called out, on opening the back door. 'Just hand me the keys and I'll put the luggage in the boot. This is Marina, by the way, all the way from Sydney, Australia.'

'How do you do, miss?' the chauffeur said, lifting

his cap in greeting as she climbed in and settled in the most comfy brown leather seat.

They exchanged a smile in the rear-vision mirror. 'His Lordship was over the moon when he found out you were coming, miss. It's ever so good of you to do what you're doing.'

'That's nice of you to say so, but I'm only doing what anybody would do, under the circumstances.'

'I wouldn't say that. I wouldn't say that at all.'

'What wouldn't you say, William?' the man himself asked, on joining them and handing back the keys.

'That not everyone would do what this pretty lady is doing for Rebecca. Or come this far to do it.'

'You're quite right. I wholeheartedly agree with you. Straight to the apartment, William.'

'Very good, My Lord.'

His Lordship stayed well over on his side of the roomy back seat, Marina noted, which was a relief. There was something about being confined in a car with him which was even more disturbing than ogling him from behind, or conjuring up erotic little scenarios in her head. Their enclosed closeness meant she could not only see him. She could smell him.

No matter how often Shane showered he still smelt slightly of sweat and horses. This man smelt of something very expensive. An exotic, spicy scent which teased the nostrils and made you think of crisp clean air and pines covered in snow, of cool white sheets and freshly washed bodies and...

Oh, my God, I'm doing it again!

Marina wrenched her mind back from the abyss, turning her head away from the inspiration of her erotic thoughts and that damned cologne he was wearing. She stared out at the suburban London street and the rows of identical houses, and tried to pull herself together.

'You mentioned your mother died of cancer...'

Darn it, he was speaking to her. She would have to turn her head back and look at him.

She did so. Slowly. Nonchalantly. 'Yes, that's right,' she said, and their eyes met. He really did have riveting eyes, she thought. The blue was as intense as their expression.

'Was it leukaemia?' he asked.

'No. She died from skin cancer. A couple of months back. Melanoma. It took her fairly quickly after it was diagnosed. Though it's never quick enough, is it?' she added, her heart contracting at the thought of her mother's suffering.

'And your father? How is he coping?'

'My father died when I was just a baby. A horse he was breaking in threw him into a fence. Snapped his neck. That's why I have no brothers or sisters.'

'Your poor mother.'

'Oh, Mum coped. Mum always coped. She was very strong. Very brave.'

'Her daughter takes after her.'

Marina shook her head. 'I wish I did. But let's not talk about me. I want you to tell me about Rebecca and her background.'

'What would you like to know?'

'Oh…everything, I guess.' She was very curious about the child, plus how she came to have such a young great-uncle.

'It's only a half-hour drive to Mayfair at this time of day,' he said a touch ruefully. 'I doubt I can fit the Winterborne saga into such a short space of time. But I'll try. Though I'll keep it down to the relevant details and leave whatever family skeletons I can in the closet. I want you to think well of us.'

'I already think well of you,' she said, before she could bite the words back.

But it was true. Aside from the unfortunate physical attraction, she *did* think well of him. This was no selfish man sitting across from her. A selfish man would not have personally taken himself in to Heathrow airport at five in the morning. A selfish man would not have given a hoot if his chauffeur had arthritis. A selfish man would not love a little girl as he obviously loved his great-niece.

His smile was ironic. 'You don't really know me, Marina.'

She shrugged. 'A man is known by his actions.'

He nodded slowly up and down. 'I'll try to remember that. Now where was I? Oh, yes. Rebecca…'

Marina soon realised she could listen to the Earl of Winterborne talk all day. He had a wonderfully rich voice. And perfect vowels. She would never have imagined perfect vowels could fascinate her, but they did. The whole man fascinated her, if she was truthful. As did his story…

It turned out that James had not been born to be

the earl of Winterborne. That honour had gone to his brother, Laurence, who was an amazing twenty years his elder.

This Laurence had apparently been a bit of a wild one, given to gambling and living the high life. Unfortunately, his father, the Earl, had dropped dead of a coronary soon after his elder son turned twenty-one, so Laurence had inherited the title at a young age.

Admittedly, Laurence had startled everyone by marrying almost immediately, but any hope that marriage would settle him down and make him face the responsibilities associated with his title, plus running the family estate, had soon evaporated—mostly due to his choice of wife.

Joy was the youngest daughter in a family of four daughters, all of them renowned for their wildly ambitious and social-climbing natures. With the high-flying Joy by his side, Laurence's life had been even more flamboyant and extravagant than ever. They'd gambled together, travelled abroad, skied, shopped and partied. They'd hardly ever been at Winterborne Hall, which was a relief to Laurence's mother, who was still grieving for her husband while trying to bring up a young son at the age of forty-five.

The birth of a daughter, Estelle, two years after their wedding, had done nothing to change the jet-setting lifestyle of Lord and Lady Winterborne. They'd merely installed their new-born baby at Winterborne Hall with a nanny and taken off again.

Because of their closeness in age, Estelle had been more like a little sister to James than a niece, and

although he and his mother had done their best to fill
the gaps of love in the child's life Estelle had grown
up feeling neglected and abandoned by her parents.
She'd always imagined it would have been different
if she'd been a boy, and heir to the title, but James
doubted it. His brother didn't give a fig about what
happened to the title after he was gone.

Estelle had eventually left home and begun taking
drugs, then, after her parents cut off her allowance,
had paid for her habit through selling herself on the
streets.

By this time James had been at university, at
Cambridge, and Estelle would occasionally contact
him when she was desperate for money. He would try
to talk some sense into her but to no avail. It had only
been when she'd fallen pregnant a few years later—
father unknown—that he was able to talk her into going home.

She had, and, with her grandmother's help, had
stayed drug-free till she'd given birth to her daughter,
Rebecca. Less than a month later, however, she had
died of an overdose of heroin. She was twenty-
five—two years younger than her uncle James.

Rebecca's grandparents, who'd still been leading
self-indulgent lives, had been no more interested in
their granddaughter's well-being than they had in their
own daughter's. A nanny had been hired and that was
that. Unfortunately, when Rebecca was only one year
old, her great-grandmother had passed away, and,
with James leading his own life in London by then,

little Rebecca had seemed doomed to grow up even more lonely and neglected than her own mother.

Fate had stepped in, however, when her grand-parents were killed on the ski-slopes of Switzerland during an avalanche two years back, making James the new Earl of Winterborne. He'd taken over the reins at Winterborne Hall, plus the guardianship of his then five-year-old great-niece, and had just brought some real love and happiness into the poor tot's life when she'd been diagnosed with leukaemia.

Her existence over the last couple of years had consisted of nothing but doing the rounds of specialists, stays in hospitals, chemotherapy and sheer misery.

'So you can see,' Rebecca's amazingly young great-uncle finished up, 'she's been having a real rough time of it.'

'It goes like that sometimes, doesn't it?' Marina commiserated. 'It doesn't rain but it pours.'

Just then the rainclouds parted and a ray of sunshine pierced the passenger window, landing in Marina's eyes. She blinked, then laughed softly. 'I hope that sun's a good omen. I think it might be, you know. I mean...what were the chances of finding a near-perfect match with Rebecca? One in a million?'

She turned her head towards her co-passenger, and caught him staring at her with those intense blue eyes of his. 'I would say that just about describes you,' he said in a serious tone.

Marina's heart flipped over at the compliment. Her laugh felt strained. 'What a flatterer you are, My Lord. You'll turn my head if you don't watch it.'

He said nothing, and she found his silence even more unnerving than his penetrating gaze. What was he thinking? Feeling? Was it merely curiosity about her which made him stare so? Surely the attraction couldn't be mutual, could it?

She swallowed, and struggled to think of something to say. *Anything*.

'Are…are we far from Mayfair?' she asked, even when she already knew the answer. They were skirting a large park, possibly Hyde Park, and the streets were heavy with traffic even at this early hour. Some time back the rows of suburban houses had given way to impressive old buildings, mostly made of a greyish stone. Not a glass and concrete skyscraper in sight anywhere.

'Not far,' he said. 'I take it you haven't been to London before?'

'Actually, I have. A couple of years back. Came on a shoestring and did what touristy things I could afford. Saw the changing of the Guard at Buckingham Palace, and Madame Tussaud's and the Tower of London, not to mention all the museums and galleries. The free ones, that is,' she laughed.

'Did you go to the theatre?'

'Heavens, no. Too expensive.'

'I'll take you, if you like.'

She shot him a sharp look, but there was nothing in his face which suggested anything but politeness.

'Oh, I…er…I don't think I'll really have the time, do you? Not if I'm to go down to Winterborne Hall as well.'

His eyebrows lifted in surprise. 'You mean you'll actually come?'

'I...well...you said you wouldn't take no for an answer.'

His laugh did not sound particularly happy for some reason. 'But I never for one moment thought you'd succumb to that kind of male pressure.'

What a provocative expression, she thought. Succumb to male pressure. It conjured up the image of an attempted seduction and an almost unwilling surrender.

Marina could not help staring into his face again, for some hint of his feelings towards her. But there was nothing to go on. He had a habit of holding his facial features in that stiffly autocratic fashion which bespoke things like ancestral pride and honour and arrogance, but nothing of any personal emotion. If he was attracted to her on any physical level, his body language did not show it.

While some deep feminine instinct rang a warning that perhaps it was not wise to go down to Winterborne Hall, suddenly wild horses would not have kept her away. She wanted to see his ancestral home, wanted to see him in it, wanted to sleep in one of those dozen bedrooms—if only to spend the night fantasising over the Lord and Master of Winterborne Hall.

'It's not a matter of succumbing to male pressure,' she said firmly, 'but deciding for myself that I would really like to see Rebecca's home. Still, I can only spare a couple of days. I really need to be getting back to *my* home as soon as possible.' Back to the real world, she told herself ruefully. And away from this fantasy one, complete with fantasy man.

'You must be missing your fiancé,' he said. 'What was his name again?'

'Shane.'

'What does he do for a living?'

'He helped my mother run her riding and dressage school. He's quite marvellous with horses.'

'I see. But what is he doing now that your mother has passed on?'

'Just the same. It would be a shame to let all my mother's work go to rack and ruin. She built up a good business with plenty of clients. And her horses are simply the best.'

'But that's not what *you* do, is it?'

Marina was startled by his intuitive comment. 'Why do you say that?'

'Your hands, for one thing. It's also obvious you don't spend much time in the sun.'

She stared down at her soft, pale hands, which were resting lightly in her lap. She was unnerved by the sharpness of his observations. What else had he noted about her? Could he look into her mind as well, see all those appalling thoughts she'd been having about him?

Her fingers linked together and pressed down hard. 'You're quite right,' she said a little stiffly. 'I'm a teacher.'

'A teacher,' he repeated, and smiled a strange little smile. 'Yes, I can see you in front of a class. But not boys,' he added wryly. 'You would distract boys far too much. You teach at a girls' school, I gather?'

Marina was rather rattled by his comments. For, while the use of the word 'distracting' suggested he found her looks attractive, this fact seemed to slightly annoy him. Was this because she was an engaged woman? Would he perhaps have adopted a different attitude to her if she'd been free to accept...to accept...what?

A romantic tryst while she was down at Winterborne Hall?

Marina found such a thought breathlessly exciting. It was with difficulty that she reminded herself she had developed an overheated imagination since stepping off that plane. For all she knew, the Earl of Winterborne was just making idle and polite conversation to pass the time while in her company. His tendency to an occasional sardonic remark could be caused by boredom. It was a sobering thought.

'Actually, you're wrong this time,' she told him crisply. 'I do teach boys. Boys *and* girls. I'm a primary school teacher. I have a class full of nine- and ten-year-olds. Or I did. I've taken compassionate leave till next term.'

His smile was accompanied by a drily amused gleam in his eyes. 'Ahh. But boys of that age are not boys at all, just wild little savages. I was thinking of the slightly older species, which begins to appreciate the difference between boys and girls. And how old are you, exactly, Marina?'

'Twenty-five.'

He said 'ahh' again, as though highly satisfied with her age.

The green saloon turned down a narrow street at that point, angling between cars parked down one side, then turning into an even more narrow and slightly cobbled lane. The brick buildings on either side were three storeys high, with doors which opened straight onto the street. So did the windows. Only the window boxes spilling with brightly coloured flowers gave some relief to the austerity of the architecture.

'These are mews,' His Lordship volunteered, on seeing her glance around.

'Oh, yes, I've read about them. They used to be the royal stables, didn't they?'

'Not all of them royal, but certainly once belonging to London's wealthy. They've all been converted to apartments nowadays.'

'They must still be expensive, being so close to the city.'

'I dare say. This one's been passed down through the family. I inherited it when my father died. It might normally have gone to the eldest son but I think Father wanted to keep some of the estate out of Laurence's spendthrift hands. As it was, my brother did his best to bankrupt the estate.

'But I shouldn't be telling you any of this,' he muttered, seemingly irritated with himself for doing so if his expression was anything to go by.

He frowned and leant forward to tap his chauffeur on the shoulder. 'William, just let us out here at the door.'

The car stopped next to a large brown wooden door with a brass knocker and doorknob. Geraniums and petunias blazed from hanging baskets at eye-level on either side.

'And give me the key for a moment. I'll get Miss Spencer's luggage. No, don't argue with me. I know how painful your knee is. If I'd had my way you'd have stayed home in bed and I'd have driven myself this morning. Now, after you've parked the car, come inside for some breakfast. We don't have to leave for the bank for another hour at least.'

The chauffeur sighed heavily. 'You spoil me, My Lord. Your brother would not have—'

'My brother is no longer in charge, William. I am.'

Which, clearly, he was.

Magnificently and mercifully.

Marina saw then that it was not just the Earl's handsome face which had captivated her. Or his tall, well-proportioned body. It was the man himself. His whole person. His character. But especially his compassion.

'Wait there till I help you out,' he ordered her peremptorily, before climbing out himself.

But she didn't wait there. That wasn't her way. She was out of the car and standing beside the passenger door by the time he brought her suitcase around.

His smile carried wry reproach. 'I thought you said that when in Rome you were going to do as the Romans do?' he chided.

She shrugged, smiling. 'My mind is willing, but my flesh is weak.'

He stared at her for a second, then shook his head again. He seemed to be always shaking his head at her. 'I doubt anything about you is weak, Marina,' he complimented her, though in a cool voice. 'Like most Australians, you flout the old-fashioned ways and traditions for the sometimes foolish habits they are. But you haven't encountered our Henry as yet. Believe me when I warn you things in this apartment are done Henry's way, or not at all!'

# CHAPTER FOUR

'WHO'S Henry?' Marina asked after the car had moved off.

'He's my valet. He used to be the butler at Winterborne Hall.'

'Oh? What happened? Didn't he work out?'

'He worked out very well for over thirty years. But my brother forcibly retired him when he turned seventy—packed him off to live out his days at the damned gatehouse like a broken-down racehorse banished to a far paddock.'

It was clear by his irritable tone that he had been furious at his brother for this action.

'Henry was still fit for service,' Lord Winterborne swept on. 'All he had wrong with him was the odd touch of gout. The poor old chap would have died through sheer neglect and boredom, so I brought him up here to London—told him I needed some company, plus someone of his experience to put some well-needed order into my wretched existence.'

'And was your existence really wretched?' Marina asked, thinking to herself how typical it was of this man to do such a thing, to care about a poor old retired servant.

'Lord, no. I was in my twenties and living the life of Riley! It was Henry's existence which was wretched. I quickly came to regret my foolishly generous gesture. Henry took me at my word and, indeed, put order into my life.' He rolled his eyes at the memory.

'How did he do that?' Marina was intrigued.

'You have no idea.'

'No, I don't. Tell me. I'm dying to know.'

His glance was drily amused. 'You have a compulsively curious nature, I think. But you're also very easy to tell things to, do you know that?'

'Yes, I've been told that before. Children come up to me in droves when I'm on playground duty to tell me their problems. And I'm always getting beseiged by little old ladies in buses and trains, and even supermarket queues. Maybe they're just lonely and need someone to talk to, but why it's always me they choose to pour out their hearts to, I have no idea.'

'It's your eyes,' His Lordship said as he looked right into them. 'You have understanding eyes.'

She flushed slightly under his compliment and his direct gaze. 'So...er...what did Henry do?'

'What *didn't* he do?' His Lordship grumbled as he reached out and rang the doorbell. 'Firstly, he converted my reading room into a gym, into which I was dragged every morning for a work-out. As a man whose only exercise before that had been turning on my computer and moving chess pieces, believe me when I tell you I was in agony for weeks. I nicknamed one particularly diabolical piece of equipment "the rack".'

'Well, it seems to have done you good,' she said. 'You look very fit.'

'I've suffered for this body, I can tell you.'

Marina thought the suffering well worth it. 'So what else did he do?'

'Changed my daily diet to a boring menu of low-cholesterol, low-salt meals. I hardly enjoy eating any more, except when I crack and go to a café and order the fattiest, most cholesterol-ridden pie I can find!'

Marina laughed while His Lordship scowled.

'But his crowning achievement was to bully me into giving up smoking. God knows how he managed that!'

'He sounds quite wonderful,' Marina said.

His Lordship finally smiled a wry smile. 'Oh, he is. But he took some getting used to on a daily basis. Now I wouldn't be without him. For one thing he plays a damned good game of chess. Of course, he *is* getting a little slow on the stairs,' he added, frowning at the still closed door. 'He turned seventy-seven last birthday.'

The door opened at that precise moment and Henry stood there, impeccably dressed in a butler's morning uniform of grey striped trousers, black jacket, white shirt and pale grey tie. He was even wearing white gloves. Marina noticed that his black shoes were polished as only a butler or a sergeant-major would polish them.

He had clearly once been a handsome man. And tall. But his back was not as straight as she imagined it had once been, and his steel-grey hair was thin and receding well back from his high forehead. He still looked a darn sight younger than seventy-seven.

Controlled grey eyes swept over her with a bland but all-encompassing glance which revealed nothing of his impression or his opinion. His coolly unreadable gaze returned to his employer.

'The plane was on time, My Lord?' he asked, somewhat starchily.

'Slightly early, Henry. And this is Miss Marina Spencer.'

Henry inclined towards her with a stiff nod, which could have been rheumatism or just his way. 'How do you do, Miss Spencer?'

'She will insist on being called Marina, Henry,' His Lordship said drily as he ushered her inside, depositing her suitcase by the door. 'So we might as well get that out of the way up front.'

'I see. Very well. How do you do, Miss Marina? Welcome to London. I have your coffee perking, My Lord, but have prepared a proper English breakfast for the young lady. You are not one of those impossibly modern young people are you, Miss Marina, who only drinks coffee for breakfast?' This with a sidewards glance of ill-concealed exasperation at his employer.

Marina only just managed not to laugh helplessly. He was so pompous and prim, he was adorable. 'Heavens, no, Henry,' she replied, the corners of her mouth twitching. 'Where I come from, some of us can eat a horse for breakfast.'

'I am most relieved,' he sniffed, and, picking up

the heavy suitcase with incredible ease, turned to lead the way.

It was a most gracious way too, Marina noted, following across a spacious black and white tiled foyer where, many metres above, hung a huge chandelier. Ahead curved an elegant staircase, covered in the middle by a wide strip of deep forest-green carpet whose pile was so plush it would be like walking on velvet in your bare feet. Sheer luxury!

Not that she'd expected anything less from a Mayfair apartment owned by an earl. Her eyes darted around as she mounted the steps.

The walls were wood-panelled up to a point, above which lay very English-looking green and gold striped wallpaper. The crystal and brass light fittings were splendid, as were the undoubtedly antique furniture pieces resting in various nooks and crannies.

'I have put Miss Marina in the Rose Room, My Lord,' Henry said on their way upstairs.

'Very good, Henry. Oh, and Henry, William will be along for a bite to eat shortly. Since I know he'll refuse to eat with Marina and myself, give him something in the kitchen. And make sure he's taken his medication. His arthritis is very bad this morning, poor devil.'

'I will see to it, My Lord. Breakfast will be served in fifteen minutes in the morning room. I thought Miss Marina might wish to freshen up first after her long flight.'

'Indeed I would, Henry,' she agreed, smiling when she realised she was talking like these two now.

'What's so amusing?' His Lordship muttered by her side as they trailed after Henry.

'Me,' she said. 'I think I'm beginning to do what the Romans do.'

'Not you, Miss Marina,' he teased drily.

'Oh, yes, me. Next thing you know I'll be taking tea in the afternoon and eating cucumber sandwiches.'

'And what do you usually have in the afternoon?'

'Just coffee.'

'I'm a coffee man myself. Especially in the mornings. I drink at least three cups.'

'So I gathered. What happened to the low-salt, low-cholesterol meals?'

'I can only tolerate so much of that. And definitely not first thing in the morning.

'I'll leave Marina to you now, Henry,' he said more loudly, once they reached the landing on the first floor. 'I'll see you in the morning room in fifteen minutes, Marina. Henry can tell you where it is. And don't be late or he'll be after you with a long stick.'

He turned and strode on, up a second but smaller flight of stairs which Marina deduced led to his private domain on the next floor.

'Very funny, My Lord,' the valet called after him in a droll tone.

'Don't take any notice of him, Miss Marina,' Henry continued as he led her down a wide hallway lined with massive gilt-framed paintings which looked as if they belonged in the National Art Gallery. 'His Lordship likes to rag me. It's a hang-over from his adolescent days when I was butler at Winterborne Hall and Master James alleviated his boredom by playing practical jokes on the staff—mostly on me.'

Marina found such a scenario impossible to imagine. Lord Winterborne surely had never been a boy, let alone a practical joker!

Henry stopped at a cream-painted door on their right. He opened it wide, then stepped back to wait for Marina to go in first.

She couldn't help it. Her breath caught as she walked through the doorway.

'Oh, Henry!' she exclaimed. 'This is the most beautiful bedroom I have ever seen. Why, it's fit for a queen!'

Her eyes were wide as they took in the delightfully feminine decor with its rose theme. Roses were everywhere, all of them in shades of pink. Tiny, pretty roses. They covered the wallpaper and matching curtains and bedlinen. They might have been overpowering if the room had been small, but it was immense.

Besides the sleeping arrangements, there was a cosy and intimate sitting area in front of a cream marble fireplace, with cream and gold silk-covered armchairs facing it. Fresh roses in pinks and yellows filled an elegant vase on the undoubtedly antique lacquered coffee table. The carpet was a deep cream, and the bed, though not a four-poster, was queen-sized with brass bed-ends.

The dressing table and matching stool in the corner nearest the bed were the epitome of feminine frippery, with their rose-covered throw-overs and exquisite gilt-framed mirrors. Fresh roses again filled an exquisite crystal vase sitting on the right side, while on the left lay a silver and crystal vanity set. In the middle sat three crystal perfume holders.

Marina's bedroom in her mother's house back home was very pretty, and mainly pink as well, but nothing compared to this.

Henry carried her suitcase over and placed it carefully on the cream-painted ottoman at the foot of the large bed. 'I don't think this room has ever had a real queen stay in it overnight,' he replied seriously, to her remark. 'But I do recall a countess or two. And Lady Tiffany always sleeps here when she stays overnight in London.'

'Lady Tiffany?' Marina asked innocently enough as she walked over to look through the window down at a small courtyard below.

'I'm sure you'll meet Lady Tiffany during your stay, Miss Marina. She comes up to visit Rebecca often. She's the youngest and only remaining child of the Duke and Duchess of Ravensbrook. His Lordship's next-door neighbours. Her poor brother, who would have been the next duke, was tragically killed in the Gulf War. He was His Lordship's best friend. His Lordship is very fond of the Duke and Duchess. *And* of Lady Tiffany. She's a dear, sweet girl.'

It finally got through to Marina that she was being told something very deliberately by Henry. When she looked around at him he was standing ramrod-straight at the foot of the bed and his gaze was steely.

'His Lordship and Lady Tiffany are planning to announce their engagement at Lady Tiffany's twenty-first birthday next month,' he stated, then just waited, as though expecting her to say something.

She found she could not for a few seconds.

Her dismay was out of all proportion to the situation and her feelings—which, after all, were just silly, secret feelings. They weren't really real. How could a girl like herself entertain real feelings about a man like Lord Winterborne? To do so was to waste both her emotions and her time. He was always going to be matched with someone like this Lady Tiffany.

Marina dredged up a smile even while her heart was not having a bar of her common sense reasonings.

'That's wonderful,' she lied. 'James is a fine man. And I'm sure Lady Tiffany is as sweet as you say. I must give her my congratulations if and when we meet. Actually, I'm going to be married myself next month, Henry.'

She could not help but see the relief in the valet's face. It both irritated and puzzled her. What had he been thinking? And why? He'd only known her for a few minutes and had only seen her with His Lordship for the same. What had passed between them which would make this old man think she was a threat to his employer's marriage or happiness? Had he overheard their light exchange on the staircase and interpreted it as a sign of growing intimacy?

Even if that were the case, did this starchy old gentleman's gentleman think she was a bold, amoral hussy, who would try to steal another woman's intended?

Whatever, she felt offended at Henry's judgement

of the situation. She might have entertained the odd fantasy or two about her host in her head, but she would never try to put any of them into action.

*Pull the other leg, Marina,* that awful voice piped up in her head. *His Lordship could get you into bed in no time if he put his mind to it.*

*Enough!* Marina's conscience intervened. *I am not that type of girl!*

*Maybe, but is he that kind of man? Most men are, you know.*

'That's good news, Miss Marina,' Henry was saying while this argument raged in her head. 'Very good news indeed. I hope you'll be very happy. Now, I'll leave you to freshen up. The morning room is on the ground floor. Just take the hallway under the staircase and it's the first door on the left.'

He bowed stiffly, then withdrew with a slightly self-satisfied smile hovering around his mouth.

Marina glared after him till he shut the door. Then she did the strangest thing. She slumped down on the side of the rose-covered bed and burst into tears.

# CHAPTER FIVE

'YOU do look tired,' His Lordship said as he started his third cup of coffee. 'And you've hardly eaten a bite.'

Marina gave him a wan smile across the six-seater circular table which was set as elegantly for breakfast as for a formal dinner party. The white tablecloth was starched linen, the cutlery silver, and the crockery fine white gold-rimmed china.

The whole room was not quite as formal as the rest of the house, however, and looked out onto the court-yard Marina had spotted from upstairs. Painted in creams and yellows, and with the sun shining through the tall windows, it would have been a bright and welcoming room if Marina had been in a bright and welcoming mood.

'You're not hungry?' His Lordship asked.

Marina stared blankly down at the breakfast she herself had selected from the superb sideboard buffet, which offered a huge range of hot food not to mention a choice of cereals plus freshly squeezed orange juice.

She'd sat down with a glass of the orange juice and a plate on which she'd unthinkingly deposited two poached eggs, two strips of bacon, a sausage, one slice of grilled tomato and several mushrooms. So far she'd only managed the orange juice and half a slice of bacon. The four slices of toast which Henry had placed on the table in a silver toast rack remained untouched, and she hadn't got round to the brewed pot of tea Henry had set before her.

Her appetite had totally deserted her, her earlier bout of irrational weeping leaving her feeling oddly fragile.

'I do think I need a sleep,' she admitted. Sleep would mean she could not think. She didn't want to think any more, about Shane or about this man opposite her. She certainly didn't want to think about the youthfully sweet and undoubtedly beautiful Lady Tiffany Ravensbrook.

'Are you sure you're up to being admitted to the hospital this afternoon?' His Lordship asked.

'Yes, of course I am,' Marina practically snapped. 'So, please, don't even *think* of putting it off. I don't want any delay in doing this. If I'm still asleep when you get back from the bank after lunch, just wake me up.'

He'd told her when she'd first sat down about his position as vice-president at one of London's largest merchant banks and how he had to go there after breakfast for a few hours. He also had a lunchtime appointment. 'Or, better still, have Henry wake me beforehand so I'll be ready when you come home.'

Marina could see by his frown that he was puzzled by her shortness. She sighed, and tried to remember that none of this was his fault. He'd not let her think by word or deed that he felt anything for her but an understandable admiration and gratitude for what she was doing for his great-niece. She was making a right fool of herself.

As for Henry...he was just a suspicious and dirty-minded old man!

'I'm sorry, James,' she said, then blinked her astonishment at herself. 'Oh—oh, I mean...Your Lordship.'

His grin was lopsided and heartstoppingly charming. 'So you've cracked at last,' he said, blue eyes glittering with amusement. 'I wondered how long it would take. From now on it will be James and nothing but James. And I will *not* take no for an answer.'

She couldn't help it. She smiled back at him, and melted all over. 'Very well...James.'

Henry *would* walk in at that moment, with her smiling with fatuous helplessness at His Lordship. And, *worse*, James was smiling back at her and looking at her for all the world as though he found her the most desirable, delightful and interesting woman. He then topped off the awkward and easily misunderstood situation by looking up at Henry and saying, 'Marina's finally consented to calling me James, Henry. For a minute there I thought I was going to have to put up with His Lordship for the next ten days or so.'

'Ten days or so, My Lord?' Henry echoed stiffly, a frown gathering. 'I booked Miss Marina's return flight for next weekend. I was assured by the hospital she would be ready to travel by then.'

'Yes, yes, no doubt she will be,' James said as he scraped back his chair and stood up. 'But I'm going to take her down to Winterborne Hall for a few days before she goes back to Australia. Don't worry, I'll have my secretary change the booking.'

Henry frowned some more. 'Have you forgotten, My Lord?'

'Forgotten what?'

'Lady Tiffany will be away in Italy around that time?'

James tossed his linen napkin down on the table. 'No, Henry,' he returned, with a sharp edge in his voice. 'I haven't forgotten. I am not taking Marina down to Winterborne Hall to visit with neighbours. I am taking her there to show her the countryside and Rebecca's home.'

Marina's swift intake of breath heralded her realisation that the Earl of Winterborne had no intention of telling her he was on the verge of becoming engaged, or of letting her path cross with his intended. Her shock was only superseded by exciting flashes of wicked speculation. Was this deliberate on his part? Did Henry know his employer better than she did? Did the Earl of Winterborne have a secret passion for redheads?

Maybe his marriage was to be one of convenience on his part? Marina speculated some more. A merging of money, breeding and titles. Maybe he meant to have women on the side, ones he momentarily fancied, ones he would keep secret from his naive young bride. It wouldn't be the first time such things had happened in those circles. And what better choice of a passing bed-partner than a woman who would return to a far-off land at the end of the affair—a woman committed to someone else…?

Marina stared up at James and wondered if his acutely observant mind had picked up on her unexpected but quite intense desire for him. Was he already planning her seduction? Plotting to have her while his fiancée was overseas?

It was obvious Henry feared as much. And he would know the nature of the beast better than herself.

Marina's emotions swung from a breathtakingly intoxicating excitement over such a prospect to an acute disappointment in the man she'd thought perfect. Perhaps she should not have put him on such a pedestal. After all, he was a human being, not a saint. A man, not a machine.

'But surely Lady Tiffany would like to meet Miss Marina,' Henry persisted.

With this reminder of James's intended, Marina decided with more reluctance than she would have liked to admit that she could not possibly be a party to any potentially sordid sexual games, if that was what His Lordship had in mind.

'Yes, and I'd like to meet *her*,' she tripped out brightly. 'Henry tells me you and this Lady Tiffany are getting engaged shortly, James.'

There was no doubting that His Lordship glared at his valet at this piece of news. But only for a second. Just as swiftly he laughed, but when he looked back at Marina, his expression was wry.

'You *did* say people liked to tell you things, didn't you? Believe me when I say it's not like Henry to gossip so. What will you tell her next, I wonder?' This with another caustic glance the valet's way.

'Possibly that you're the best Earl of Winterborne in a hundred years,' Henry volunteered, with a po-faced expression. 'That you're a good man, with a great sense of responsibility, loyalty and tradition. And that you love your niece's child, Rebecca, as if she were your own daughter and would do anything to make her future a lot happier than her past.'

'My, my, Henry. Do you think any mortal man could live up to such a glowing testimonial?'

'I think you'll try, My Lord.'

James nodded slowly up and down, a rueful smile pulling at his mouth. 'You are a sneaky old man, Henry. What alternative do I have in front of our guest but to agree with you?'

'I know that, My Lord.'

'You know too much, Henry.'

'I have lived a long time, My Lord. Your brother would have said too long.'

'My brother may have been right,' James muttered, before throwing Marina a parting smile. 'See how he browbeats me into behaving myself? Have a good sleep, Marina. I'll be back with the car to pick you up at two-thirty. Henry, make sure Marina eats some lunch before that. We don't want her relying solely on hospital food, do we?'

'Certainly not, My Lord.'

And then he was gone.

Marina stared at the empty doorway and wished her

heart was not beating so, despite feeling intolerably heavy.

'You haven't eaten much of your breakfast, Miss Marina,' Henry said as he gathered James's coffee cup and pot onto a tray.

'I…no, Henry. I'm sorry,' she said dully. 'I seem to have lost my appetite for some reason.'

'Perhaps you are nervous about what lies ahead of you in hospital, miss,' he said, with a gentleness in his voice she hadn't heard before.

'Perhaps, Henry.'

'Maybe you'll feel more like eating after a nap.'

'Maybe.' Her chin began to quiver and tears filled her eyes anew. Panic that she was about to disgrace herself had her rising abruptly from her chair and, in doing so, bumping the valet's arm. The silver tray he was holding slipped from his grasp and crashed to the polished floor, smashing the coffee cup and spilling the remains of the coffee from the pot.

'Oh, dear heaven!' she exclaimed, her face stricken. 'I'm so sorry, Henry. I'm such an idiot!' She squatted down immediately to help clear up the mess, but the incident seemed to have opened the floodgates of her very mixed-up feelings and tears started to stream down her face.

'Oh, God,' she choked out, when Henry's expression showed he was aghast at this display of emotion. 'I…I'm just tired,' she tried to explain through sobs. 'I'll be all right…in a…in a little while.'

Henry took the broken crockery from her shaking hands and placed it back on the floor, then he helped her back upright. The arms he curved around her heaving shoulders were incredibly gentle. 'You just need a good sleep, Miss Marina. Come. Let me help you upstairs.'

'Th-thank you. You're...you're very sweet,' she said as he did so.

'It's no trouble. And you're the one who's sweet, Miss Marina. I can see why His Lordship is so taken with you.'

She blinked up at him through blurred eyes, halting to dash away the remains of her tears and withdraw from the valet's steadying arms. They were halfway up the staircase and Marina leant against the mahogany balustrade, gripping it tightly with one hand.

'Why do you say that, Henry?' she demanded to know, if a little shakily. 'There's nothing between His Lordship and myself. Goodness, we only met this morning. He's getting engaged next month, and, as I said, I'm going to be married myself around the same time. If you think for one moment I would entertain the thought of some kind of illicit liaison with His Lordship while I'm over here, then you're very much mistaken!'

Henry seemed unfazed by her indignant outburst.

'That's as may be, Miss Marina, but I know what I know and I see what I see. His Lordship *is* taken with you. Make no mistake about *that*. Experience has shown me that there are not many ladies who remain indifferent to him once he turns on the Winterborne charm.'

Marina didn't know what to say. She wasn't sure

if she was flattered by Henry's conviction or afraid of it. As for herself…it was pointless to deny the obvious: she was more than charmed by the Earl of Winterborne. It seemed crazy that such a thing could happen in such a short space of time. But it had. Her feelings for Shane seemed positively lukewarm in comparison to the feelings James could engender in her with just a look.

But that still didn't mean she was prepared to hop into bed with him.

'I have met plenty of Australians in my time,' Henry went on. 'I know they don't like people to…er…beat around the bush? So I hope you won't take offence over what I am about to say.'

Marina had a feeling she would. Henry might have met a good few Australians in his time, but he didn't seem to have much regard for the moral fibre of their women!

'His Lordship is going through a difficult time at the moment. He is under stress with what is happening to Rebecca. As I said earlier, he adores that little girl. On top of that, his relationship with Lady Tiffany is not the sort of relationship he is used to with his lady-friends. As such, he may be extra vulnerable at the moment to an undoubtedly real but ultimately passing attraction. Do you know what I am saying?'

Marina wasn't sure she did—till she recalled Henry telling her earlier that Lady Tiffany always slept in the rose room when she stayed overnight. Since this modern young woman was on the verge of engagement to James, wouldn't it be more natural if she spent the night in *his* bed?

The realisation that James was not sleeping with his soon-to-be fiancée should not have thrilled Marina.

But it did.

'I see you *do* understand what I'm saying,' the valet stated stiffly, his eyes not perfectly at peace with the pleased expression on her face. 'Maybe I have said too much,' he muttered.

Marina swiftly wiped the hint of satisfaction from her lips. 'No, no, Henry, you did the right thing,' she hastily assured the well-meaning valet. 'And I will give you the benefit of an equally straight-talking reply to your concerns. I promise you I have no intention of doing anything to compromise His Lordship or his coming marriage while I am over here. I *like* James very much. Okay. I *more* than like him. I think he's bloody fantastic. How's that for a good old Aussie expression? But I'm no fool. Neither am I a woman of easy virtue.'

'Miss Marina! I never meant to imply that—'

She waved him to silence. 'No, I realise that. But you do seem to think I have no will of my own in this matter. You seem to think James would only have to proposition me and I would forget my own fiancé back home and jump into bed with him. Not so, I assure you,' she insisted, and hoped valiantly that it was so.

'I also think you have overestimated James's feelings for *me*. Why should he be so taken with me? I'm not all that good-looking, for one thing. There must be plenty of ladies in James's social circle much more beautiful and glamorous. And *willing*, Henry,' she added pointedly. 'Do you honestly think a man as attractive as James could not indulge himself sexually any time he liked, if that was what he wanted?'

'I never said that was what he *wanted*,' Henry argued back.

'Then what *are* you saying?'

'Just that sometimes people get caught up in a combination of situations which work against their natural decency. I have *not* overestimated His Lordship's feelings for you, I assure you. I do think, however, that you *under*estimate your own attractions, Miss Marina. Aside from your delightfully feminine shape, you have a luminescent kind of beauty which shines from your face and your eyes. As for your hair...it has a touch-me colour and quality which any man would find hard to ignore.'

Marina coloured as her hand fluttered up to touch her hair. 'You exaggerate. Surely?'

'Not at all. About anything. I *know*, Miss Marina, what my Jamie-boy likes.'

She stared at the valet, aware he had deliberately used this old nickname to show her how well he *did* know his one-time boyish charge.

'You're frightening me, Henry.'

'I hope so, miss. For I would not like to see you go home with a broken heart. At the moment it is only beating as any woman's heart might beat faster when a man such as His Lordship flatters her with his

attention. Take care not to let it beat faster for any
other reason. Go down to Winterborne Hall with His
Lordship by all means. But be on your guard against
the temptation to forget where you are and who you
are not.'

Marina drew herself up straight, her pride and
self-esteem sending a gleam of righteous anger into
her green eyes. 'I am as good as the next person,
Henry.'

'I agree with you, Miss Marina. But you are not
the lady whom His Lordship is going to marry. Even
if you were madly in love with him—which seems
unlikely at this stage—would it be in his best interests
to ever acquaint him with that fact? Would you not
show your love better by leaving him in peace to
make a marriage he is not only committed to but
which he will go through with regardless of his own
feelings?'

'Are you saying he doesn't love this Lady Tiffany?'

'I am saying no such thing. Of course he loves
her—just as he loved her brother. He also gave his
word to that brother, Miss Marina. He promised his
best friend as he went off to war that if anything happened to him he would look after his little sister. This
marriage is a sacred duty, in His Lordship's eyes, and
one which he was quite happy to carry out...till this
morning...'

Marina felt very disturbed by what Henry was im-
plying. 'But I haven't done anything!'

'Only been your lovely natural self, Miss Marina.
I am not imparting any blame. I agree, things haven't

progressed too far as yet, but I see the warning signs. Don't forget I have been His Lordship's valet for the past seven years, and I know his ways well. I can practically read his mind in matters of the opposite sex.

'He is not used to leading a celibate life, and his hormones may get the better of his conscience—especially if a lady whom he finds attractive is to be constantly alone in his company and will keep looking at him as though she thinks he's...what was the term? Bloody fantastic?'

Marina's sigh was as heavy as her heart. 'I get the picture, Henry.'

'Then you will stay out of the picture?'

Her chin lifted. 'I will do what is right.'

Whatever that was. She had no idea at that moment. She didn't think like these people. She didn't live her life by rules of stiff tradition and sacred duty. She went with her heart. And her heart at that moment told her she just might *be* madly in love with the Earl of Winterborne.

Stranger things had happened. If love at first sight did not exist then why had it been written about for centuries? Whatever her feelings for James turned out to be, she certainly knew that she could not marry Shane now. What she felt for him definitely wasn't love. He'd filled a need in her life when she'd been wretched and lonely, then confused her with his expert lovemaking.

Marina resolved to do the right thing and break her engagement when she returned home. She would soften the blow for Shane by giving him both the horses and the business name of the riding school he'd helped build up with her mother. Somehow she didn't think he'd be too upset with the arrangement.

As for doing the right thing at this end of things... That was up to James, wasn't it?

# CHAPTER SIX

'YOU'RE looking much better,' James said as he handed her into the back seat of the green Bentley for the ride to the hospital, supposedly only a ten-minute trip—fifteen if the traffic was bad.

Marina had earlier secured Henry's approval for her choice of a plain black suit for the occasion, as well as the way she'd done her hair, its bright mass of red-gold curls held back at the nape of her neck with a plain black clip.

The valet hadn't actually said anything, but she was beginning to read his facial expressions, as subtle as they were. Approval rated the barest nod of his head on first sighting, plus the minutest gleam in his steely grey eyes.

Henry would not have approved if he'd been able to read her mind. Or her heart. She'd been breathless with anticipation for James's return from the moment she'd woken, hardly able to wait to see him again, to *be* with him again. Lunch had been stuffed down, not because she'd felt hungry but because James had ordered her to eat. Marina suspected she would do anything Lord Winterborne ordered her to do.

'You obviously had a good sleep,' he added when he climbed in beside her.

She tried not to stare, but she'd forgotten, even in

67

that short space of time, just how handsome he was. Mindful of Henry's warnings, and her own infernal conscience, she hoped nothing of her innermost feelings showed in her face, or her eyes.

But how wonderful it would be—just once—to feel free to lean over and press her mouth to his, to look deep into his eyes and tell him how her heart raced whenever he was near, how heaven, for her, would be to spend just one night with him.

Her mind drifted to such a scenario, but this time, strangely, her fantasy was no longer of an explicitly erotic nature. She saw them as just lying together, naked, yes, but simply looking at each other and touching each other tenderly, long, stroking caresses, without tension, without the distraction of the flesh aching for release.

And then she realised she was thinking about how it would be with him...afterwards. Shane always rolled over and went straight to sleep. Marina knew, instinctively, that James would not do this. Not with *her*...

'That's a most attractive perfume you're wearing,' he muttered, the softly spoken compliment snapping her back to the present. 'I don't recognise it.'

She simply could not look at him. Not at that moment. If she did, she would surely undress him with her eyes and blush awfully. 'It's called True Love,' she said, and turned her head to stare through the passenger window.

'Ahh. A gift from your fiancé?'

Her head whipped back to deny she had a fiancé

any more, not in her heart, and very soon not in reality. But she could not bring herself to say the words. Marina found this distressing, because deception was not in her nature. She wondered if she was deceiving James for his sake, or hers. Henry's warning about going home with a broken heart had been a fair one. Men like James didn't break their engagements for girls like her. They took them as mistresses, not wives.

For all Marina's saying she was as good as the next person, in the circles James moved in relationships had different rules. Hadn't her own upper-crust mother had to run away to Australia to be with the man she'd chosen to marry, just because he was of common descent?

'No, it belonged to my mother,' she said curtly, her lips pressing together in annoyance at her thoughts.

He stared at her primly held mouth for a long moment, then turned his own head away. It was a slow and rather arrogant gesture, his nose and chin lifting. 'I must buy Tiffany a bottle,' he said, the words a dagger to her heart.

*Idiot,* came that sneering voice she hated so much—mostly because it did not let her pretend.

*He couldn't have spelled it out more clearly,* came a second, equally frank opinion.

*Well, at least you know the score now,* was the third, and least scathing comment.

Marina tried to blank her mind, but it was impossible. The voices railed on, calling her all sorts of insulting names and adjectives. Although emotionally harrowing, Marina's mental warrings usually left her strengthened in will-power. Such was the case this time.

'I think, perhaps,' she said straight away, before she could change her silly mind, 'it would be better if I took that return flight Henry booked for me next weekend.'

That handsome head jerked round and their eyes clashed. His were furious, hers widening with shock at his instant and very fierce anger. 'What, in God's name, has Henry been saying to you?' he bit out.

Her guilty blush betrayed both herself and Henry. But the obscenity James muttered under his breath was even more betraying. For it outlined that James was, under his lordly manner, just a man, a mortal man with feelings and failings like any other.

'Interfering old fool,' he muttered. 'He thinks he knows it all when in fact he knows nothing. *Nothing!* What has he told you? Tell me! I must know.'

She didn't know what to say, for she was walking a minefield here. As she'd told Henry, there had been nothing between herself and James. At least, nothing spoken, and from what he'd just said about Lady Tiffany, and buying her a bottle of True Love, the valet might very well have jumped to all the wrong conclusions.

'He...Henry that is,' she began carefully, 'only has your best interests at heart...'

James snorted. 'He's living in the Dark Ages. That man has no concept of what life is like these days.'

Marina was startled when James suddenly slid

across the seat towards her and took her hands in his.
She shrank back from him into the corner, her eyes
rounding on his intense and far too close face. Her
heart was immediately pounding. Her lips parted
slightly as hot, panting breaths puffed from her lungs.

She was embarrassingly aware of William behind
the wheel, just a couple of metres away, blithely ignoring what was going on. Was that because this type
of thing happened all the time when His Lordship had
an attractive woman in the back seat with him? Henry
had implied James had once been a ladies' man.
Maybe he'd never given up the tag. Maybe he'd
merely moved his romantic rendezvous from his
apartment to his car!

'My God, what *has* he said to you?' he rasped, on
seeing her reaction. 'No, you don't have to tell me. I
can guess. I never could hide anything from Henry.'

'H-hide?' She had begun to tremble at his nearness.
His scent enveloped her, as did his powerful male
aura. A yearning shuddered through her and she found
herself leaning towards him. Closer. Closer.

His fingers tightened around hers. He stared down
at them, then began to lift them towards his mouth.

'No!' she choked out.

He closed his eyes for a few seconds. On opening
them, he sighed and placed her hands back in her lap.

'I do apologise, Marina. I got carried away for a
moment. I didn't mean to, I assure you. But you are
an incredibly beautiful woman. And so darned desirable! I told myself all morning that I would not, *could*

not, entertain such thoughts about you. You're going to be married, as I am.'

'But I'm not,' she whispered, then gasped in self-horror.

His eyes lifted. Pained, beautiful blue eyes.

'You're not…what?'

'Not…not going to be married,' she confessed shakily. Having said this much, she felt compelled to elaborate. 'I was already having doubts before I came. The trip away has cleared my mind, and now…now I know I can't go through with it.'

He just stared at her, his horror almost as great as her own at this conversation. 'Not because of *me*, I hope,' he groaned, with a wealth of distress in his voice.

She said nothing, but his telling words sent tears pricking at her eyes. Henry had been so right. She would be going home with a broken heart. All she could ever mean to James was a passing fancy.

His fingertips on her chin turning her slowly back to face him sent a shiver of agonised desire all through her. It did things to her conscience which would afterwards shock her.

Yes, touch me, she willed wildly as their eyes met. Kiss me. Make me yours, at least this way. I don't care if you don't love me, I tell you. I don't care…

'Dear God,' he whispered, his face shaken as he stared into hers. His hand dropped away and he withdrew from her across the seat, his fingers raking his hair as he did so.

He fell broodingly silent, leaving Marina to her

guilt and her remorse. She wished now she'd never said a thing. It had been wrong of her. And wicked. She'd been warned, but she hadn't heeded that warning. She'd blindly gone ahead and as good as told James she was his for the taking. Henry had practically begged her not to put temptation in his path and what had she done? Told him she'd broken her engagement then looked into his eyes like a love-sick cow.

She felt sick with shame.

She had to *do* something—undo the damage which had been done.

'You're mistaken,' she said quietly into the thickening silence, hoping William was concentrating on the traffic. He seemed to be, as it was horrendous. 'My decision has nothing to do with you, other than that you showed me the kind of man I would like to marry. As I said, I was already having serious doubts about Shane before I left Sydney.

'I will not deny I am attracted to you. You're a very handsome and charming man, James, as I'm sure you are well aware. Henry sensed this...attraction...between us, and it worried him. But an attraction can stay just that, can't it?' she told him, with far more conviction than she was feeling. 'We don't have to act on it. We can just be friends, can't we?'

His eyes were sardonic as they turned to her. 'Not if you look at me as you did a moment ago.'

She swallowed, then steeled herself. 'Granted. But you were touching me at the time. If you give me your word as a gentleman that you will keep your hands off, I will give you my word as a good Aussie girl not to do anything equally provocative.'

His laugh was rueful. 'I've met some not so good Aussie girls in my day.'

'And I've met some not so gentlemanly gentlemen,' she countered. 'But they are other people and this is us. I would like to think we have a sense of honour. I know I have.'

He sighed. 'How unfortunate.'

'You don't mean that, James.'

'No,' he said wearily. 'I don't suppose I do.'

'And I think we will just forget my going down to Winterborne Hall. That would not be a wise move.'

'True.'

'Now I would like to put my mind and energy back on the reason I came over here in the first place,' she said as a large hospital came into view on their right. 'We seem to have arrived and I happen to be feeling quite nervous.'

He glanced over at her and his expression carried sincere regret. 'What a selfish bastard I am,' he murmured. 'Yes, of course you must be nervous—as must Rebecca. Yet here I am, consumed with my own pathetic needs. I am so sorry, Marina. For everything. Forgive me.'

'There is nothing to forgive. Things happen sometimes which have no rhyme or reason.'

'Do they? I'm not so sure. I have come to hold the view that things are written, that fate has plans for all of us.'

She wondered if he was talking about his brother's death, as well as his best friend's. Did he believe he'd been fated to become the Earl of Winterborne so that he would be in a better position to take care of his best friend's family? It was a romantic idea, but Marina held no such views on death. When you'd seen someone die of cancer it was hard to believe in anything like that.

James shrugged off a frown and leant forward, tapping William on the shoulder. Thankfully, the chauffeur had had the radio playing and did not appear to have been listening to them.

His head twisted round a little. 'Yes, My Lord?'

'Let us off at the front entrance, William, then go and find a park. I will be taking Marina in to meet Rebecca and staying a while to visit. Wait for me in the foyer and I'll find you when I come down.'

'Very well, My Lord.' If he'd heard anything of what had gone on, he gave no indication of it.

Marina popped out of the back seat, unaided, while James collected the overnight bag Henry had lent her from the boot. It was a snazzy little red leather number, and easily accommodated her nightwear, toiletries, plus some casual clothes.

When James joined her on the top steps of the hospital entrance and put his hand lightly on her elbow, she automatically shot him a warning glance. He rolled his eyes but took his hand off.

'This is ridiculous,' he muttered from beside her on their way through the huge glass doors.

'Maybe,' she returned crisply. 'But it's the way it's going to be.'

'You're a hard woman.'

'Not at all. I have a feeling you're spoilt where the opposite sex is concerned. Not enough women have said no to you in the past! But you're not that irresistible, Your Lordship.'

'Oh, my God, we're not back to that, are we?'

'We certainly are!'

He muttered an expression under his breath which she doubted would have found favour with Henry.

Marina almost smiled. There was something rather satisfying in taking the reins where this situation was concerned. She wasn't a teacher for nothing. Bossiness came naturally to her where little boys were concerned, and underneath she had a feeling there was still a little boy in the Earl of Winterborne.

Unfortunately, there was also a big boy. A very good-looking, utterly appealing and incredibly sexy big boy!

But she wasn't going to think about that, was she? And she wasn't going to listen to that awful voice in her head any more, the wickedly dark one which kept telling her she could have this man if she wanted to. That she could go down to Winterborne Hall and spend every night in his bedroom, then wing her way back to Sydney with no one the wiser—least of all Lady Tiffany Ravensbrook, whom Henry had kindly informed her would be in Italy!

## CHAPTER SEVEN

THE first thing Marina saw when James directed her towards Rebecca's bed in the children's ward was not the small child propped up against a mountain of pillows, but the young woman sitting on the side of the bed with a book in her hands.

She was the most beautiful girl Marina had ever seen. Not just attractive. Not just pretty. Beautiful. Breathtakingly beautiful.

Straight, shoulder-length blonde hair. Skin like porcelain. A perfect profile. Full soft lips. A slender, fragile-looking body.

Marina knew at once who she was.

The girl looked up at their approach, and her eyes matched the rest of her. Large hazel eyes, thickly lashed and immediately smiling at James—as was her lovely coral-glossed mouth.

But it was the child in the bed who spoke first, the bald-headed, deathly pale, unbelievably thin child, whose big green eyes looked too large for her face.

'Uncle James!' Rebecca exclaimed, excitement bringing some colour to her hollow cheeks. 'Look, it's Uncle James, Tiffany. And he's brought my Marina with him!'

Marina was startled but touched by this term of endearment. And yet it was true, wasn't it? She *was*

Rebecca's Marina. They were going to become
bonded as few people could be. Her own flesh and
blood was going to save this brave little girl's life.
She just knew it would!

Marina came forward and held out her hands to the
child, who took them straight away, without hesita-
tion. Out of the corner of her eye, Marina was aware
of the exquisitely lovely Lady Tiffany standing and
giving James a peck on the cheek. They also began
whispering to each other. She steadfastly ignored the
jab of jealousy and gave all her attention to Rebecca,
sitting down and giving her a big hug.

'Oh, Uncle James!' Rebecca cried afterwards.
'She's so pretty. And she has hair the same colour as
mine! When I have hair, that is,' she added, a little
self-consciously.

'You'll have hair again, my pet,' Marina said
softly, and took the child's hands again. 'In no time
at all, you're going to be feeling *so* well.'

'Yes, I know. Uncle James rang me this morning
and he said we're going to do it tomorrow. I can't
wait!'

'Neither can I.'

'The doctors said it won't hurt. Of course I'll be
fully asleep, but you have a choice. You can have a
general anaethestic, if you like, or just a local. I think
you should have a general,' she advised in all seri-
ousness. 'Then you won't have to worry whether it
hurts or not. You see, doctors *always* say things won't
hurt, but mostly they do a bit.'

Marina's heart twisted at this seven-year-old trying

to reassure *her*, the adult. She was like a little adult herself. But that was what pain and sickness did to one. It made you old before your time.

She'd seen it before in other children, when she'd gone to the hospital to visit her mother and stopped in sometimes at the children's cancer ward. Her heart had just wept for the poor, brave little darlings who'd seen more misery in their short lives than most people had in a lifetime.

'I think I'll be a coward and have a general,' she confided quietly. 'I'm not brave like you.'

Rebecca giggled. 'Did you hear that, Uncle James? Marina thinks *I'm* brave. Oh, that's so funny. I'm not at all brave. I cry all the time when they put those horrid needles in me. I *hate* needles,' she whispered to her new friend and confidante.

'Well, heavens to Betsy, of course you do!' Marina said indignantly. 'What self-respecting girl would *like* needles. Yuk! I shudder just to think of them.'

Rebecca crowed with laughter. 'Oh, but you *are* funny. And you talk funny, too,' she said, obviously referring to Marina's accent—though it wasn't as broad as most, due to her elocution lessons. Marina had always thought she sounded rather British. Clearly she didn't.

'But I like it,' Rebecca announced. 'And I like you too. She's smashing, isn't she, Uncle James?'

The arrival of a nurse wanting to do a routine check of Rebecca's vital signs gave James the perfect excuse not to answer. Unfortunately it also meant Marina had to finally face the girl he was to marry.

Gathering herself, she stood and turned, flinching at the sight of James's arm around Lady Tiffany's slender waist.

On second sight the girl was even more lovely. She was wearing cream cotton trousers with a cream and fawn striped vest-style top; the simple outfit screamed the sort of style money could not necessarily buy. The girl had class and elegance which had been bred into her. It was inherent, as was the way she held herself, so upright, and with a proud little tilt of her perfect little nose.

She was, for want of a better word, a lady.

'I'm so glad I had the opportunity to meet you,' the lady herself said, after James had introduced them. 'I think it's marvellous what you're doing. Rebecca is such a darling. I only wish I could be here for her tomorrow, but I have to fly to Italy this afternoon. In fact, I must be going shortly, James.

'Now don't go saying you'll come with me to the airport. That's silly. You stay here and visit with Rebecca. I've ordered a taxi. I only dropped in for a while on my way. I have to go to Rome to be in the wedding party of one of my cousins,' she explained to Marina with the sweetest of smiles.

Marina's own smile felt plastic. Why couldn't she have been a bitch? An upper-class snob with a snooty attitude instead of this softly spoken and obviously very *nice* girl.

'I don't really want to go, but I'm obliged. Worse, I'm having to go several days before the actual wedding to have my bridesmaid dress properly fitted. It's not even a nice dress,' she added laughingly. 'And it's purple! Can you imagine me in purple?'

'You'd look lovely in anything, Tiffany,' James complimented her.

Tiffany gave him such an adoring look Marina wanted to cry. This girl not only loved him, she was *besotted* by him. A quick glance at James's face showed more than mere affection for the girl in return. His gaze was meltingly indulgent and definitely loving.

They looked splendid standing there as a couple, she as fair and delicate as he was dark and strong. Marina could see why Henry was so protective of the relationship. Lady Tiffany would make a perfect Countess, the perfect partner for the best Earl of Winterborne in a hundred years.

'I agree,' Marina said quickly, to cover her dismay. 'With your hair and complexion, any colour would suit you. I would be a disaster in purple. Scarlet doesn't do much for me, either.'

Lady Tiffany laughed softly, and Marina tried not to pull a face. But there was just so much perfection she could take. Why couldn't the infernal girl have had yellow incisors, or molars full of metal, or an overbite? Why did her laugh have to show two flawless rows of immaculate pearly whites?

Marina herself had had to suffer years of braces to correct her own dental shortcomings.

Physical perfection in James she could admire and lust after. But not in this exquisite creature who was going to become his wife, but whom Prince Charming had not yet acquainted with his undoubtedly virile flesh.

Why *was* that? Marina puzzled all of a sudden, and with a vehemence alien to her normally pragmatic personality.

Surely she couldn't still be a *virgin*? Not in this day and age, not at nearly twenty-one and certainly not looking like *that*!

But the more Marina stared into those big hazel eyes the more she became convinced that Lady Tiffany was totally untouched by male hands.

*Totally!*

There was an unknowing innocence in her face, and in those eyes. The glances she sent James contained nothing of naked desire and everything of a blind and almost adolescent hero-worship. That peck she'd given him on the cheek bespoke the affection more of a sister than a lover.

What in God's name was James waiting for? For them to be officially engaged? Surely he didn't expect to hold out till his wedding night! That was archaic, and totally unnatural when two healthy young people were in love. He should be making love to her all the time. Good grief, if *she* were engaged to him then she would not—

Marina caught herself up short.

*But you're not engaged to him, Marina,* that awful voice piped up. *Whether Tiffany is a virgin or not is none of your business. The same applies to the current status of His Lordship's sex life. Or are you thinking of taking up the slack, so to speak? Of giving the poor dear chap some well-needed comfort while the ice-princess swans off to Italy, naively leaving her intended behind in the clutches of the evil Aussie seductress?*

'Look, Uncle James!' Rebecca said delightedly. 'Marina's daydreaming, just like me!'

Marina pulled herself quickly together and walked over to the bed again. 'Nothing wrong with daydreaming. I have a lot of fun in my daydreams.'

'So do I,' Rebecca replied happily. 'When I daydream, I'm all grown up and beautiful, with hair just like yours. I'm never ever sick. And I'm married to a wonderful man like my uncle James and I have lots and lots of children. I don't like being an only child,' she finished, her lips pouting.

Marina's heart turned over at the child's dream, which rather echoed her own. What she would not give to be in Lady Tiffany's shoes! 'Being an only child has *some* good points,' Marina said kindly, sitting down on the edge of the bed. 'For one thing it develops your imagination and your self-sufficiency.'

'What's self-suff...suffish...' Rebecca pursed her lips in frustration. 'What you said!'

Marina smiled. 'It means being able to do things all by yourself. It means being strong.'

'Uncle James says I'm strong.'

'He also says you talk too much,' James intervened. 'Now say goodbye to Tiffany. She has to go now.'

'Oh, does she have to?' the child wailed, for once sounding like a seven-year-old. 'She hasn't finished reading me the story about the princess.'

'I'll finish reading your story,' Marina offered. 'I'm not going anywhere. I'm sleeping here tonight.'

'Oh, goodie! You can go now, Tiffany.'

Lady Tiffany laughed good-naturedly. 'Such is the loyalty of the Winterbornes. But I'll bring you back a present from Italy anyway.'

'And will this Winterborne get a present too, when you come back?' James asked, giving his intended a darkly brooding look. Or so it seemed to Marina.

But the girl just laughed, seemingly unaware of the sudden sexual tension emanating from the man whose arm was around her.

'What could I possibly buy *you*, James?' she said. 'You have everything you could possibly want in that apartment of yours.'

'Not everything one wants can be bought, Tiffany,' he said.

She gave him a totally blank look.

'You'd better get going,' James said, though it sounded as though the words came through gritted teeth.

'Yes, I'd better. I'll be back next Monday. The morning flight.'

'I'll be there,' he said, with a hint of a sigh which perhaps only Marina heard.

Tiffany certainly seemed oblivious of her intended's strained state.

'You spoil me,' she said, and pecked him on the cheek again before turning to Marina. 'Goodbye,' she said with sweet politeness. 'I dare say I won't be seeing you again, which is a shame. I would have loved to find out all about you, and life back in Australia. It seems such an exciting country, and so different from England. I'd love to go there one day.'

'Then I'm sure you will,' Marina said, wishing with all her heart that she didn't like this girl so much. Then she wouldn't have to feel so guilty about the dark desires which still lurked in that treacherous mind of hers, ready and waiting to find a chink in her own armour. It was particularly perturbing that she could not wait for Tiffany to leave and fly away.

'Goodbye for now, poppet,' Tiffany directed at Rebecca. 'And good luck for tomorrow.'

'Bye, Tiffany,' Rebecca chirped back.

'Goodbye,' Marina said, guilt sending her forward to give the girl a kiss on the cheek. But when she glanced over her shoulder at James he stared at her, and his eyes carried a black frustration.

'When are you going to finish reading my story, Marina?' Rebecca asked as soon as Tiffany was gone.

'Right now, if you like.' And she picked up the book and sat down.

'Don't wear Marina out too much, sweetie,' James warned. 'Or yourself, for that matter. The doctors want you both bright-eyed and bushy-tailed tomorrow.'

Tomorrow, Marina thought with the beginnings of a nervous lump in her stomach. She wasn't really worried about anything hurting. But she did hope it would all go well. The last thing she wanted was to go home with a broken heart *and* a failed mission.

# CHAPTER EIGHT

THE bone marrow transplant went well. More than well. It went perfectly.

Marina was discharged the morning after the procedure, with the doctors glowing in their optimism for Rebecca.

Although it was too early for their little patient to show signs of rejection, the specialists were unanimous in their opinion that she had the very best chance of a complete remission, since Marina was the best donor match that could be found outside of a brother or a sister.

Marina had learned on the evening she'd been admitted to the hospital just how lucky they had been to find a match for Rebecca outside of a relative, since her blood type was not a common one.

Marina had been surprised to learn that even if Rebecca had had a brother or a sister their bone marrow would not necessarily have been compatible. There was only a one in four chance of a perfect match between siblings. Even a twin was no good, because a twin, in fact, was actually *too* perfect a match. Only by having a register with millions of names on it could it be hoped to find a match outside of the family circle.

Having had all this explained, Marina had been

asked permission for the media to be brought in and a story told about their amazing match. That way, many thousands of others might be inspired to do what Marina had done.

She'd asked James about it, and while he hadn't been thrilled with the idea, and had vetoed any cameras being shoved in Rebecca's face, Marina *had* been interviewed and a story run on the news the following day and evening.

But when several news crews were waiting outside James's apartment when he brought Marina home from the hospital on the Wednesday morning, Marina saw the Earl of Winterborne in action, with all his arrogant, autocratic anger.

Henry would have blushed at his language, but Marina found herself on *his* side, totally. She had no time for the media when they started invading people's privacy, when they crossed lines which had been clearly set out for them. Marina had given permission for *one* interview and one interview only. If they were going to start hounding her she would have to jump on an even earlier plane than Sunday's.

Which was exactly what she told James after he'd routed the rabble and bundled her into the safety of his apartment.

'You will do no such thing!' he snapped.

Anger became him, she decided, looking at his flashing blue eyes and furiously stubborn jawline. The suit he was wearing became him too. It was pale grey and a silk blend, teamed with a crisp white business shirt and a blue-striped tie the same colours as his eyes, which were light blue in the centre rimmed by a darker navy.

Or so she'd found out after staring into them at length.

Every time they met anew now, they stared at each other, as though the time apart had been agony. Despite the distraction of her hospital stay and the media problem, Marina found her feelings for James were escalating rather than abating. And becoming intensely physical once more. Any admiration or respect for James as a person was being buried underneath an avalanche of desire for him as a man. She didn't know how much she could stand before the compulsion to touch him would overwhelm her.

He seemed under similar stress. During his several visits to the hospital he'd made a point of not getting too close to her, especially when she'd been in her nightwear. There had been no touching of any kind, no goodbye pecks, just an unsettling series of smouldering stares. Unfortunately, during the incident with the media outside, he'd had to take hold of her waist to shepherd her through the small crowd of aggressive journalists and photographers. His arms around her had rattled both her composure and his.

'You will stay the full week,' he ordered angrily. 'And you will let me take you to the theatre!'

'I will not,' she refused, sounding coolly firm even while her heart was racing.

They were standing in the foyer, facing each other at the base of the stairs.

'If you do not let me take you to the theatre,' he ground out, 'I will kiss you here and now.'

She just stared at him, afraid that he might, terrified that he wouldn't. For the threat, once voiced, conjured up the threatened kiss in her head. It would be hard and hungry. Not the sort of kiss she would normally like. But she would like such a kiss from him. She would like it much too much.

'Did you hear me, Marina?'

She clenched her jaw hard and prayed for salvation. 'I did, My Lord.'

He grabbed her shoulders and yanked her hard against him, scowling down into her instantly wide-eyed face.

'James,' he bit out. 'You will call me James or, by God, I will do more than kiss you.'

'James,' she whispered in a raw, shaking voice.

His face twisted as he fought the urge to do it anyway, to ravage her mouth *and* her body.

She saw the battle in his eyes and should have helped him out. But how could she when his body was pressed close to hers? When his mouth was a mere breath away from closing over hers and sending her to the hell she was beginning to ache for?

The sound of footsteps on the staircase sent them springing apart, James looking for all the world like a naughty schoolboy caught with his trousers down.

*Which they might have been shortly,* that ugly voice sneered.

Marina only just managed not to laugh hysterically. This was starting to feel like an Edwardian farce. But was *she* the heroine or the bitch? And was James the hero or the dastardly villain?

'Disgraceful,' Henry was muttering as he plodded down the last few stairs. 'Simply disgraceful!'

For a moment Marina thought he was talking about them.

'I tried to get rid of them earlier, My Lord,' he said apologetically to James, 'but they simply took no notice of me.' He turned to give Marina a small smile of greeting. 'And how are you feeling, Miss Marina? His Lordship told me everything went splendidly at the hospital.'

'The doctors are very optimistic, Henry. And I feel quite well, except for a tiny throbbing in my right hip. Nothing that some aspirin and a cup of your lovely brewed tea won't cure.'

'I will leave you in Henry's capable hands, then, Marina,' James said abruptly. 'William is waiting outside to take me on to the bank. I will get my secretary to make a booking for us on Friday evening for a show. Your hip should be better by then. Would you like to see a play or a musical?'

To argue at this point would be to tell Henry too much. 'A play would be lovely,' she said levelly.

He nodded and was gone in a flash, leaving Marina to stare longingly after him for a moment. She turned to find Henry watching her with those all-seeing grey eyes of his. Suddenly she saw red.

'Don't start, Henry,' she said rather sharply. 'And do stop worrying. I'll be gone soon. Then Your precious Lordship will be out of danger.'

She went to brush past the valet, but he stayed her with a soft but firm hand on her shoulder. Her eyes blurred slightly as she looked up at him.

'It's not just His Lordship I worry about,' he said gently. 'I would hate to see a lady as fine and lovely as yourself hurt in any way. His Lordship is a good man, but, as he said himself the other day, he is only mortal. And any mortal man could not help but find you desirable, Miss Marina.'

Marina might have coped with Henry's reproach. Or even some more of his dire warnings. But not his sympathy and kindness. 'Oh,' she cried softly, her hands fluttering up in a futile effort to stop the tears from flowing. 'Oh, Henry!' And she threw her weeping self against his broad but stiffly held chest.

For a second he froze, but then his arms went round her. Surprisingly strong yet gentle arms. 'There, there, Miss Marina,' he soothed. 'It's not as bad as that. Surely?'

'Yes, it is,' she sobbed. 'I love him, Henry. I love him so much.'

He froze. 'Don't say that, Miss Marina. Don't even *think* it.'

'I can't help thinking it. It's all I think about.'

'And you're all *he* thinks about lately, I'll warrant,' Henry said drily. 'But it's not love which spurs *his* mind, child. It's those blasted Winterborne hormones.'

'But I have hormones *too*,' Marina moaned.

'Miss Marina!'

Henry immediately put her aside, as though he was

in imminent danger of contamination after this appalling confession.

Marina blinked her astonishment—till she realised that men like Henry were not of the modern world. They were an anachronism. They actually believed sex was a male prerogative. A male flaw, perhaps, to be tolerated and hopefully controlled.

'I'm sorry to shock you, Henry,' Marina said, 'but it's not just James who thinks about sex. You might be surprised to learn that there are a lot of ladies these days who think about sex! So please, for pity's sake, don't worry so much about James taking me to the theatre. Or taking me anywhere in public. It's infinitely safer than our being in this apartment together, even if we do sleep on different floors and have you here as watchdog.'

Henry's spine straightened and his chest puffed up with indignation. 'I am no spy!' he protested.

'No, not a spy. More of an interfering guardian angel. Don't take offence, Henry. I do appreciate your good intentions. And I fully understand the predicament I find myself in.

'If it helps to put your mind at rest, I met Lady Tiffany at the hospital on Monday and I think she is one of the loveliest and nicest girls I have ever met. I would never deliberately do anything to hurt her, even if I don't think she's the right girl for James. She is far too young, far too naive, and far too sweet. James will walk all over her, which means he'll be bored to tears in no time flat.'

Henry was frowning, as though some of what she

was saying made sense, even if such thoughts had never occurred to him before. 'You don't think they'll be happy together?' he asked worriedly.

'No, I don't. They seem the perfect romantic pair on the surface, and they do look good together. But will it work in the bedroom, Henry? I ask you that. A man like James will not be satisfied with any girl who might be daunted—or totally dominated—by his Winterborne hormones.

'In the past, wives of this ilk might have tolerated their husbands dallying elsewhere, but not nowadays. Under the circumstances, I suggest you worry over the next woman to spark your esteemed boss's carnal desires, and not me. *I* won't be any danger to his marriage from Australia, will I? Even if I *have* decided not to go through with my own marriage, which would be a similar disaster!'

Wrenching off her engagement ring and clenching it in a tight fist, Marina marched off up the stairs, leaving a frowning Henry behind. She kept her chin up, but her heart had sunk to an all-time low. For, despite her bold and impassioned speech, she knew Henry was right about the most important factor. James didn't love her. He just wanted her.

Come next week, he probably wouldn't give her another thought ever again. He would go on to marry Lady Tiffany, and if they weren't happy then it would have nothing to do with a certain spinsterish teacher living out her days in Sydney.

# CHAPTER NINE

JAMES finally settled in the roomy back seat of the white stretch limousine. William and the Bentley had been given the night off, it seemed, to be replaced by this huge luxury vehicle with its plush red upholstery, black windows and equally opaque privacy screen, which was at that moment sliding into place.

When they were completely alone—unable to be heard or seen by the driver—James turned to look at her across the seductively lit cabin.

'You look…stunning,' he said.

Marina's hair was up and she was wearing black again, the only outrageously expensive little black dress in her wardrobe, which had been a must to bring. Mostly because it did not crush. When she'd packed it, never in her wildest dreams had Marina thought she would wear it for a man.

But she was very definitely wearing it for James. It was cruel of her, she knew. For it could be a very provocative dress when worn with the minimum of underwear. And she was wearing it with *no* underwear other than a pair of sheer black Lycra pantyhose which had built-in panties.

The material was a silk crêpe and the style very simple. A basic sheath, it was severely cut in at the shoulder, with the front of the bodice gathered onto a round collar which was covered with black jet beads. The collar did up at the back of her neck with a hook and eye. There was no zipper, just a slit down the middle of the back from neck to waist. Mostly this slit stayed demurely shut, but just occasionally it gaped apart as she walked—or climbed into cars— with the expanse of bare back displayed shouting the absence of any bra or other undergarment.

Not that any man with twenty-twenty vision needed to look at her *back* to know she was braless. Marina was by no means a busty girl, but she had nice B-cup breasts, which were high and firm, with perky nipples which announced their naked state under the thin black material with all the subtlety of Henry's dire warnings.

'Thank you,' Marina said coolly. She leant back in the relative safety of her distant corner to survey James at her leisure. He was wearing a superb black dinner suit with a white dress shirt and a black bow tie. He looked magnificent. Dignified and handsome. A true lord in every way.

But, lord or no lord, he could not take his eyes off her. And Marina revelled in that fact.

I'm punishing him, she realised. For not loving me but for still wanting to take me to bed. I'm trying to make him suffer.

And he *is* suffering. I only have to look into his eyes to see it, to watch the way his fingers curl into tight balls when he's with me. And to see the dark rings under his eyes at breakfast every morning.

'Henry tells me you rang home today,' he began, after the limousine had moved off.

'Yes, that's right.'

She declined to say any more.

Shane had not even asked her how the transplant had gone, or how Rebecca was. All he'd wanted to know was when she'd be home and was she sure none of this was costing them any money. He'd never sounded more selfish or less loving. She'd also heard a girl laughing in the background who sounded awfully like Heather, the twenty-year-old who helped with the horses every weekend.

What had Heather been doing in the house, and on a weekday? she'd wondered for some minutes after hanging up.

The answers were not nice ones.

'Did you tell him you weren't going to marry him?' James asked curtly.

'No.'

'Why not? I notice you've taken off his ring.'

'I might change my mind back again,' she lied, and he shot her a look which made her want to laugh. He didn't want to marry her, but he didn't want her to marry anyone else. It would almost be funny if it wasn't so infuriating.

'My views on love and marriage have changed somewhat since being over here,' she continued icily, giving in to the compulsion to punish him further. 'I see no reason why us commoners can't operate on the same level as the upper classes. Marry with our heads and not our hearts. Shane will do very well by the horse business I inherited from my mother. And there is the added bonus of his being a more than adequate lover. You have no idea how talented a rider he is, in every way.'

'Don't,' James rasped. 'For pity's sake, Marina.'

Her shame was instant, but pride demanded she didn't back down. 'Don't what?'

'Don't torture me so,' he groaned.

'And what have you done to me these past two days?' she challenged. 'Avoided me like poison, even when I ran into you at the hospital when I went to visit Rebecca with Henry. You didn't even come home for dinner last night. Then you make an appearance tonight to take me out, looking like Prince Charming on his white charger, trying to seduce me with extravagant compliments.'

'They aren't compliments,' he said with a weary sigh. 'They're true. You *are* stunning. And I only stayed away because I could not bear seeing you all the time—just as I could not bear *not* to do this tonight.'

'What? Try to seduce me?'

He glared at her. 'That's the pot calling the kettle black, isn't it? I could accuse *you* of trying to seduce *me*, dressed as you are. Still, I'll recognise your right to dress as you please if you will recognise my right to react to the end result as any red-blooded male would.'

She laughed. 'What a pathetic excuse! Why don't you just say it, James? Spell it out. Tell me what you had in mind for tonight *before* you saw how I was dressed.'

His eyes narrowed upon her. 'I had nothing in mind,' he said tautly. 'I had become quite resigned this past week to being the complete gentleman till the bitter end.'

She laughed. 'Sure. That's why you ordered this little number.' And she waved her hand around the inside of the limousine. 'Blind Freddie could see that this is just a boudoir on wheels! What's the catch, James? Have you got a standing order for one of these whenever you take a girl to the theatre, or wherever else you take them? The ones you want to impress, that is.'

'I did not order this car,' he bit out frustratedly. 'Henry did.'

'Oh, sure.'

'It was either this or a taxi. William put the Bentley in for servicing and it wasn't going to be ready in time. You're quite wrong about my intentions, Marina. Now stop it, will you? I can't bear any more tonight.'

For a moment Marina felt guilty. It had been a hell of a week for him. She knew how worried he'd been about Rebecca. It was to be thanked that the early signs were so good. Rebecca had looked marvellous this afternoon. She'd been chirpy and cheeky, a very good sign. And the doctor had said her early blood tests were more than hopeful.

But, Rebecca aside, they really did have to sort this out.

'Well, if I'm wrong about your intentions, then tell me what's right,' she demanded to know. 'Tell me what you feel for Tiffany. And what you feel for me,' she added, her voice breaking a little.

He closed his eyes and shook his head. 'Dear God, you won't give me any peace, will you?' He opened his eyes to turn his head and look at her again, his face full of frustration.

'I am fond of Tiffany,' he stated brusquely. '*More* than fond. I have known her for years and we are well matched. The only reason I haven't slept with her is because she doesn't want to till we're married. She has been brought up in a very...old-fashioned...way. For reasons which are complex, I would feel duty-bound to marry her even if I didn't *want* to marry her!

'I admit I've been having trouble with living a celibate existence,' he confessed, combing agitated fingers back through his perfectly groomed black hair. 'But I vowed to myself I would remain faithful, come hell or high water! I just never dreamt that my hell or high water would come in the guise of a fiery, red-headed Australian girl whose spirit and beauty I have come not only to admire but to covet as I have never coveted before!'

He glared at her, as though this was all her fault. And she *was* beginning to feel very guilty over her dress.

'I convinced myself I could endure till you left England,' he went on, blue eyes glittering with desire as they roved down her body, then up again. 'And I might have succeeded if I, too, had not received a phone call today. From Tiffany.'

Marina's heart gave a nervous little leap. 'What...what did she say?'

'She told me she wanted to wait a while before getting engaged. She said she was worried she was too young for marriage at this stage. She said she needed some time and space to think things over.'

Marina was astonished. The girl she'd seen at the hospital had clearly been besotted by James. What had happened in Italy to give her last-minute doubts?

'And what did *you* say?' she asked James.

'I said I understood, and that she was being very wise if she was at all unsure.'

It immediately crossed Marina's mind that James had not told Tiffany in return that *he* was having doubts. The way remained clear for him to marry the girl, if and when she got over these last-minute nerves.

'How very...convenient for you,' she said, a bitter taste in her mouth.

James glowered over at her. 'There is nothing at all convenient about any of this, Marina, especially what I feel for you.'

Before she could protest, he slid over the wide red seat and forcefully gathered her hands in his. 'I have never really fallen in love in my life,' he confessed. 'Not with a passion which has lasted anyway. I can't say what I feel for you is love. I only know that it is different, and infinitely distracting. Desire for you has dominated my every waking moment since the mo-

ment we met. My sleep is similarly disturbed. I can
think of nothing else but touching you, kissing you,
making love to you.'

He lifted her hands and pressed her fingertips to his
lips, kissing them feverishly. He turned over her right
hand and snaked his tongue along its palm, then up
the wrist, then along the soft, sensitive skin which led
up to the elbow.

Marina's eyes were wide upon his dark head as it
bent over her, his mouth working a shivery magic on
her arm. She sucked in a shaky breath every time his
hot, wet tongue trailed over a new and seemingly
more sensitised spot.

She would never have believed an arm could pos-
sess such erotic zones. He was moving higher now,
above her elbow, up to her shoulder and down around
the deep armhole of her dress. Her breast seemed to
swell as his mouth drew nearer, its nipple tightening.
Oh, God! *Both* breasts were responding now. Her
heart began to thud heavily and her lips parted to let
the ragged breaths escape her panting lungs.

When his head lifted to look at her, her eyes felt
glazed. He held them while he unhooked the collar
on her dress and peeled it downwards, trapping her
arms by her sides and baring her shamelessly aroused
breasts to his sight.

At last, his eyes lowered to look straight at them.

'God forgive me,' he muttered. But it didn't sound
like a prayer. More an expression of ruthless resolve.

His head began to bend and she just sat there, with
her back pressed hard against the seat and her breasts

thrust stiffly forward, her mind petrified but her flesh avidly awaiting his touch, and his tongue.

The first contact of his hands and lips on her naked flesh brought a rushing inward gasp of breath. She held it for several agonising seconds, disbelieving of the way it felt when he sucked on one breast while he caressed the other. Finally, she let the breath out in one long shuddering sigh of total surrender.

Nothing had prepared her for this, she realised dazedly. Not even Shane. For this was heaven and hell combined. Happiness, yet misery. Agony, and ecstasy. The sweetest pleasure, yet the most poignant pain.

For the man adoring her body, tormenting it, *enslaving* it, had just told her he probably didn't love her. Which was as good as saying he didn't. She would ultimately prove to be a passing passion, as all his other women had been passing passions. Only Tiffany had his heart. Tiffany, the innocent. Tiffany, the sweet. And it was Tiffany he would marry.

But it was *she*, Marina, he wanted to make love to right at this moment.

And she wanted him to. Oh, she wanted him to so much. There was an ache for him in her body and in her heart which was growing with each sweep of his tongue, with each touch of his hand.

She grew mindless with yearning, sliding slowly sidewards on the seat as he tongued her nipples into hard pebbles of exquisite torture. She moaned and writhed against the plush velvet seat, her restless legs screaming out for him to stroke them, *part* them. She ached to have him undress her further. She wanted to be naked for him. She would have done anything he asked. Given him anything he wanted.

So she was shaken when he abruptly yanked her upright. His hands felt angry as he dragged her dress up over her throbbing breasts and hooked the collar in place. Her eyes searched his for a clue as to what was going on. Why had he stopped? Had he had second thoughts? Didn't he want her any more?

Tears were just a second away when he spoke.

'Forgive me,' he said, poking a stray hair of hers back into place. 'I know how you must be feeling. But we're only seconds away from the theatre.'

Marina stared at him.

How had he known that? Had he kept an eye on his watch? Or was he a practised hand at this scenario, knowing exactly how much lovemaking he had time for beforehand, leaving his victim all primed up for the second act, *after* they came out of the theatre?

'Don't look at me like that,' he groaned. 'I said I was sorry.' And he bent to kiss her on the mouth. His first. But it was a mere apologetic peck. Not a kiss racked with uncontrollable desire. *She* was the one shaking with uncontrollable desire. James was very much back in control—of himself and the situation.

Oh, Marina, Marina, you fool. This man is a past master of such games. Didn't Henry warn you? Did you honestly think you could play with this kind of fire and not get burned?

No more, she resolved bitterly. No more.

'You're not at all sorry,' she flung at him. 'You planned this. I know you did.'

'I planned nothing,' he denied curtly. 'I give you my word. As a gentleman.'

'Then you have a strange idea of what constitutes being a gentleman. Or is it that you think I'm *not* a lady?'

His blue eyes blazed. 'What just happened between us has nothing to do with being a gentleman and a lady, and everything to do with being a man and a woman! God, if I'd planned this, do you honestly think I would be taking you into that stupid theatre at this point? I would be ordering the driver to go round in endless circles while I made endless love to you.

'I can't win, no matter what I do, can I? That's what's been so difficult about this situation from the start. Neither of us has been free to admit—and act on—how we feel. But I see now there are certain things beyond society's ideas of right and wrong. Beyond rules. What we feel for each other is one of those things. What will be will be!'

'What will be for *me* is what *I* decide!' she argued, though shakily. 'And I do not decide to be one of your passing passions! Come Sunday, I am going to fly back to Sydney, and Shane. And I'm going to forget you ever existed!'

'You think you can fight the fates, Marina?' he ground out, an angry bitterness in those beautiful blue eyes of his. 'I think not…'

She only had to recall herself a minute ago, lying half-naked and abandoned beneath him, to concede what he was saying was true. But that didn't make the truth any more palatable.

'You are not to touch me again in this disgusting car,' came her heated protest. 'You will get rid of it and take me home in a taxi. Give me your word. As a gentleman,' she finished challengingly.

He glared at her for one long, excruciatingly tense moment, then slowly turned his head away, his chin tipping up proudly. 'You have it,' he ground out.

The car slid to a halt as he spoke. The back door opened and the real world rushed back in.

Noise. Lights. Crowds.

Marina blinked and recoiled. No, she wanted to scream. No, close the door again. I take it all back. Tell the chauffeur to drive round in circles. Undress me. Make endless love to me.

Don't take me out there feeling like this! Don't make me sit next to you all night in a darkened theatre without being able to touch you. Don't torture me with this awful craving, this unacceptable, unendurable, unfulfilled desire!

But he did take her out there. He did make her sit beside him without so much as holding her hand. And he capped off the evening by taking her home in a taxi and not speaking a single word, let alone kissing her or touching her in any way.

She was in a terrible state by the time James silently opened the apartment door and waved her inside. She was on the verge of humiliating herself totally by begging him to make love to her right there on the black and white tiled floor...when Henry walked down the stairs.

'Good evening, My Lord, Miss Marina.' He nodded

sombrely towards her. 'I trust the play was enjoyable?'

The play? She hadn't heard a word of it, had no idea if it had been a drama or a comedy.

'It was excellent,' she said, and wondered how she could sound so normal when it felt as if ants were crawling all over her skin, when her breasts ached unbearably and a liquid heat scorched between her thighs. Never had Shane made her feel like this. She wanted to slap James's handsome face, rake her nails down his back, sob into his shoulder.

The valet nodded sagely. 'There is nothing like a night at the London theatre. I do apologise again for the limousine, My Lord, but it was all the hire car company could give me at short notice. William said to tell you that the car will be ready for tomorrow.'

'Tomorrow?' James echoed, frowning. 'What's happening tomorrow?'

The valet smiled an uncharacteristically wide smile. 'The hospital rang soon after you left this evening. They say Rebecca can go home for the weekend.'

'But that's wonderful!' James exclaimed.

'Indeed, My Lord. I spoke to the child herself and she was so excited. But she doesn't want to come here. She wants to go down to Winterborne Hall.'

'But of course! Anything she wants.'

'She...er...especially asked if Miss Marina could go too.'

Marina's stomach contracted fiercely.

'She can't, I'm afraid,' James said sharply. 'She has a plane to catch on Sunday.'

Henry looked a little sheepish. 'Er…I took the liberty of ringing the airline, and they are more than happy to exchange Miss Marina's ticket for Monday's flight. It seems the Sunday flight is always rather overbooked.'

James's expression was one of total exasperation. 'That's all very well, Henry, but I believe Marina is anxious to get back to Sydney and her fiancé. Isn't that so, Marina?'

Marina had to admire his ongoing fortitude. Clearly he *had* decided to fight the good fight to the bitter end, as he'd said.

But, perversely, his noble self-sacrifice only made her love him all the more. And *want* him all the more. Feeling as she did at that moment, his putting the decision in her hands appealed to her dark side, and that awful voice which would not be denied.

*He won't be able to resist you, no matter what he's decided. Not away from Henry's watchful eyes. Not down there, in one of those enormous bedrooms he's sure to occupy. Maybe he'll even have a four-poster bed…*

'I would dearly love to come down to Winterborne Hall with Rebecca,' she heard herself saying, with only the smallest quaver in her voice. 'You did the right thing about changing my flight, Henry. Don't make such a fuss, James,' she said, turning to him. 'It's only one night, after all. Shane can wait one more night.'

Their eyes locked and his widened slightly.

And then he knew. Knew what she was saying. She

would give him one night. And give *herself* one night. With him.

She watched him struggle with what she knew had to be a wickedly compelling temptation.

'It's your decision,' he said slowly, but his fists remained balled by his side.

'I've already made up my mind,' she said.

'So be it,' he said, and as he stared deep into her eyes his own were strangely cold, yet full of a dark triumph.

He was rationalising her decision, she realised. Seeing it for what it *wasn't*. A night of selfish, secret lust which would not stop either of them from forging ahead and eventually marrying others. He did not understand that she loved him with all her heart, that she would never marry any man but him, that she would go to the grave a spinster rather than settle for anything less than what she knew tomorrow night would bring.

And so the deed was done, and their fate sealed.

But was it fate? Marina wondered as she lay wide-eyed in the Rose Room bed later that night. Some kind of warped destiny which had thrown them together and forced them along this path?

She did not know. She only knew she had to do this. Call it fate. Or destiny. Or written.

Tomorrow night she would spend in James's bed.

Tomorrow night...

Her eyes slid to the bedside clock. Just after three. Would she never fall asleep?

No, she accepted with a small, dry laugh. There was no sleep for the wicked. No sleep at all.

# CHAPTER TEN

'I'M GOING home! I'm going home!'

Rebecca was bouncing up and down on the back seat of the Bentley between James and Marina.

'Do be still, Rebecca,' James said sharply.

Rebecca pulled a face at Marina. 'Uncle James only calls me Rebecca like that when he's in a bad mood.'

James sighed. 'I am not in a bad mood. I'm simply tired. Marina and I went out last night and I was late getting to sleep.'

'I didn't sleep much, either,' Rebecca said, beginning to bounce again. 'I was too excited.'

'Yes, well, I understand exactly what you mean,' was her uncle's dry remark. 'I was pretty excited myself.' And he threw Marina a scorching look over the child's bobbing head.

'Were you, Uncle James? Oh, look. There's some horses. Can I go look at our horses when I get home, Uncle James?'

'Whatever you like, sweetie. Here, come and sit up on my lap for a minute so you can see better out of the window.'

She scrambled up onto James's lap straight away, hands and nose instantly glued to the glass.

Marina resisted the impulse to feel jealous.

'You have horses too?' she asked.

He shrugged. 'I inherited them from my brother, who was racing and gambling mad. They're not riding horses. They're thoroughbred brood mares. Laurence's wife, Joy, was also mad about jumpers, and she had a whole stable of hacks. I eventually sold them, because there was no one left who wanted to ride and they cost too much to keep properly fed and stabled for nothing. But I kept the brood mares as an investment. We have plenty of good grazing land and my estate manager said it would be foolish to sell them up. He said some of the foals would bring in a small fortune. And he was right, thank God.'

'Why do you say, "Thank God"? Was the estate in financial trouble when your brother died?'

'That's putting it mildly. Laurence had run up an overdraft a mile high, the house and land had a second mortgage and several of my father's prized paintings had been exchanged for copies—the originals sold to South American millionaires. A good number of antiques had also already found their way to Sotheby's—just to support two wastrels, flitting around the world.'

'What's a wastrel?' Rebecca asked, reminding them both that there was a child listening.

'A good-for-nothing person who spends money and doesn't work,' James answered bluntly.

'Well, you're not one, Uncle James. You're *always* working at the bank. And Marina's not one because she's a teacher!' The little girl frowned, then. 'I'm not one, am I, Uncle James? I mean, I don't work, and I know it costs a lot to keep me in hospital.'

James gave the serious-faced child a hug. 'Children can't be wastrels, sweetie. That's only for grown-ups. And I wouldn't care how much it cost me to make you well.'

'You won't have to pay much more, Uncle James, because I'm going to be perfectly well in no time.'

Marina's heart turned over. She prayed that would be so with all her heart. The thought that the transplant might *not* work in the end brought a lump to her throat. She glanced out of her window, willing away tears by concentrating on the passing countryside.

It was nothing like anything you would ever see in Australia. So ordered, and so very green, despite James saying earlier they'd been having a drought. Marina had smiled at that. She doubted the English knew the real meaning of the word 'drought'. Let them travel out into the outback during a drought and see what *years*—not a single season—without rain could do. Let them see bone-dry creek-beds and the bleached skeletons of long-dead animals on the banks. Or the rotting carcasses of newly dead ones.

She shuddered herself at the image, which had actually confronted her once during a camping trip into the red heart of Australia.

Not that Australia was all like that. It was only the interior deserts which were so merciless. The capital cities and large tracts of pasturelands along the coastlines came as a pleasant surprise to some overseas visitors, who thought Australia was one big outback.

Marina especially loved Sydney, with its many

trees, its beautiful harbour and beaches. Unfortunately, her mother's house and ten-acre property was right on the rural outskirts of Sydney, quite some way from the ocean which might have tempered the soaring summer temperatures. Bringelly reached the high thirties with regular monotony during the summer months.

Marina had to admit she was not fond of such heat. Now that she was more used to England's cooler climate, she much preferred it. She'd grown to like London, too. And she certainly liked what she was seeing of the countryside.

They were on the A3 something-or-other, travelling south-west of London at considerable speed, as were all the other cars, heading wherever they were heading for the weekend. Actually, they'd been on various A3 something-or-others since leaving the M3 motorway some time back.

'You didn't want to go and see Stonehenge while you were down this way, did you?' James asked politely from his corner.

She looked over and noted that he had sensibly refastened Rebecca into her seat belt. 'No, thanks. I saw it last time and thought it highly disappointing. Maybe if you could walk amongst the stones themselves in the moonlight, you might get some of the right atmosphere. But not in broad daylight from behind a roped-off section where you walk around like sheep in a queue longer than Pitt Street.'

James laughed. 'You'll never make a tourist if you don't like sightseeing queues.'

'I agree with you. That's why my last touristy trip over here was my one and only.'

'You haven't travelled anywhere else?'

'Not outside of Australia. I've been into the outback and down to Tasmania.'

'So you haven't been to Paris? Or to Rome?'

'No.'

'Would you like to go?'

She gave him a suspicious look. Surely he wasn't going to suggest he take her? Surely not!

His smile was wry. 'Just answer the question, Marina. It's not a trick.'

'I'd go if I could go first class,' she said truthfully. 'My days of economy travel are behind me. I'm very much a once-bitten, twice-shy girl.' And make of that what you will, Your Lordship!

'I'll keep that in mind,' he murmured, and fell irritatingly silent.

Marina scowled to herself.

*See what you get for magnanimously planning to let him sleep with you tonight?* came the predictable taunt in her head. *Now he thinks you're a cheap, two-timing tramp. No, not cheap. An expensive two-timing tramp who can probably be bought for illicit weekends in Paris and Rome and God knows where. Next thing you know he'll suggest you fly back to Australia via Paris and Rome with him as tour guide. But the only sights he'll want you to see are plenty of hotel bedrooms!*

*You don't have to sleep with him tonight,* her conscience piped up. *You didn't say you would in so many words. If and when he tries to take delivery of what he thinks you promised, you can claim he misinterpreted that look, that you had no intention of doing any such thing!*

Marina closed her eyes and shook her head. She couldn't do that. The truth was that *she* wanted to sleep with *him*. The extent of her desire had kept her awake all night. Even now, inside, every nerve-ending was tingling in anticipation of the coming evening. Although exhausted from her sleepless night, she felt more alive than she ever had before.

Did James feel like that? she wondered, and turned her head just enough to look at him out of the corner of her eye.

He was wearing the most casual clothes she'd seen him in this past week. Pale grey trousers and a lightweight crew-necked sweater in broad horizontal stripes of grey and navy. His casual loafers were navy. He still looked a million dollars—his black hair perfectly groomed and that tantalising pine perfume wafting from his body.

She, herself, was wearing the tailored black trousers which went with her take-anywhere black suit, teamed today with a cream V-necked cashmere cardigan which she'd thrown into her luggage at the last moment in case the evenings were chilly. Although the sun was shining, Marina still found the air crisp.

Rebecca had insisted on wearing a rather tomboyish outfit of white T-shirt and khaki overalls, completing it with a white baseball cap.

She'd told Marina in confidence that she wasn't

going to wear girl clothes until she had hair and looked like a girl. Marina could see her point. Rebecca's bald head would have looked incongruous above a frilly dress. And she simply refused to wear a wig. She said they were hot and itchy and made her look silly!

Marina glanced up from her survey of Rebecca's clothes to find James watching her. For a moment the air between them was fraught with a sizzling tension. But then he smiled, and for a single marvellous moment Marina felt as she might have felt if they had been a real family—husband, wife and daughter—going for a drive in the countryside.

Her heart swelled with a brief burst of happiness, only to contract fiercely when she realised such a fantasy would never come true. It would be Lady Tiffany who would sit here in future years. James's wife. The Countess of Winterborne. Not silly slept-with-and-discarded Marina.

Her face must have betrayed her thoughts, for James's smile faded abruptly, to be replaced by a troubled frown. They stared at each other and Marina could have sworn that the misery in her eyes was reflected in his, that they both longed for the same thing, but both knew it would never come about.

'We're nearly there!' Rebecca suddenly shrieked. 'Look, there's the gates, Uncle James. Oh, just you wait and see this, Marina. It's the prettiest place you'll ever see!'

Marina dragged herself out of the black pit in a valiant effort to respond to the child's enthusiasm. She could not for a moment imagine that one of England's ancestral homes would be 'pretty'. But then, a seven-year-old girl would not have too many adjectives at her command. One only had to look at the ancient wall and gateposts that the more modern electronic gates were attached to in order to get a hint of what the house would be like. Dark and grey and forbidding.

They passed through the gates, which had opened and begun closing behind them as if by magic, but presumably by a remote control operated by William. On one gatepost sat a small security camera, and below, attached to the post, was a black box with a big black button which no doubt callers pressed so that they could be vetted before the gates were opened.

Just inside the gates on Marina's side stood a simply awful old house, which looked dilapidated and deserted. Although two-storeyed, it was small and narrow and gloomy. It had tiny windows and two black chimneys and ivy growing all over the walls. There was no garden to speak of. Just rambling rose bushes.

'That isn't the gatehouse Henry was sent to live in, is it?' she asked, aghast.

James nodded. 'Now you know why I had to bring him to London. The only reason I haven't had the damned thing torn down is because it's protected by a well-known charity. I ask you, what and who are they protecting it for?'

'Not me,' Rebecca said, shuddering. 'It's creepy.'

'I suppose it has a long history,' Marina ventured.

'Undoubtedly,' James agreed. 'But it is *my* gate-house, isn't it? I should be able to do what I damned well please with it! I thank my lucky stars I've been able to pull the estate out of the red, or else I might have had to hand over the place to just such an insti-tution, who would undoubtedly open the place to the public and have me spend every summer weekend standing on the front steps and smiling at those long queues of tourists you adore so much.'

Now she looked at him, *more* aghast. 'But you'd hate that!'

'Life can be full of doing things you hate,' he re-turned, and she had a feeling he was no longer talking about houses.

'I hate needles!' Rebecca piped up. 'And I still have to have them. Stop talking to Marina, Uncle James. We're coming to the pretty bit.'

The narrow, winding road dipped unexpectedly, plunging with amazing speed from open fields into a type of forest. Huge trees on either side stretched up and over, meeting in the middle of the road. The sum-mer sun attempted to pierce the canopy of leaves but could only manage a dappled light. Fractured rays of yellow danced across the shadowy avenue, creating a magical and quite fanciful atmosphere.

Suddenly they were in another world, where it was possible to believe in fairies and elves, in Robin Hood and Maid Marion, in Prince Charmings and Sleeping Beauties and happy ever after.

'It's the enchanted wood!' Marina exclaimed.

As quickly as they had descended into the fairyland

they burst out of it, and there, on a rise at the end of a long straight driveway, stood Winterborne Hall.

It wasn't dark or forbidding. Not at all. The walls were made of a creamy grey stone, the roof of a shiny grey slate. It was three storeys high, with a very wide façade.

Not a castle by any means. But a most impressive mansion. Georgian in design, Marina guessed, with its clean lines and the symmetrical placement of windows on either side of the entrance.

'What do you think?' James asked as the Bentley moved with considerably less speed over the now gravel driveway.

'It's magnificent,' she praised.

'So it darned well should be! I've sunk a damned fortune in fixing up the place after Laurence didn't spend a penny on it for years. I had the ivy stripped off the outside and the walls sandblasted last year. You don't think it's too stark now, do you?'

'Oh, no. It's breathtaking! And so are the grounds.' As far as the eye could see there were rolling green hills, like parkland, with clumps of stately trees. Closer to the house, the wide expanses of lawn gave way to more ordered gardens, with beds of flowering bushes bordering the driveway—possibly hibiscus and definitely fuchsias and oleander—all of them in full bloom. They were covered in masses of gloriously coloured flowers in reds and pinks and white.

And then there was the fountain in the middle, where the driveway parted into two and went round in a circle. It was dominated by a great bronze statue

of a chariot, horse and driver, and the circumference
of the stone pond was rimmed with bronze archers
shooting not arrows, but jets of water at the invading
warrior, whoever he was.

'I simply love it all,' Marina praised, 'but especially that fountain. There again, I do so like water.'

'Wait till she sees the lake, Uncle James!'

'Lake?'

'The grounds roll down a slight hill to a lake at the
back. There are swans and ducks, and we have a couple of boats you can take out. It's very pleasant down
there on a summer evening. There's even a gazebo on
a small point jutting into the lake.'

'I have parties with my dolls there,' Rebecca said.
'I'll show it to you after I've shown you the horses.'

'I haven't seen *any* horses yet,' Marina said, glancing around.

'They're not close to the house,' James explained.
'I have a motorised golf-cart we can use to get to
them.'

'Don't tell me you have a golf course here as well?'

'No. Just the cart. But we do have an indoor heated
swimming pool and an indoor tennis court.'

'And how many acres?' She might as well know
the whole awful truth. Might as well let it sink in as
just who and what she was dealing with here. It would
keep her feet firmly on the ground.

'Around a thousand.'

Marina knew that was a *huge* acreage by English
standards. 'My God, your next-door neighbours aren't

exactly at leaning-over-the-fence-for-a-chat distance, are they?'

He smiled. 'No. Not exactly.'

'How ever do you get to meet them?'

'At polo matches and dinner parties and balls.'

'Polo matches and dinner parties and balls,' she repeated slowly, thinking this world was a far cry from a drink at the pub on a Friday night and McDonalds and a movie on Saturday. And yet, strangely, as she looked around she didn't feel at all like a fish out of water. If she hadn't known better, she might easily have pictured herself living here, with James by her side. In a weird kind of way her mother had prepared her for just such a life. She was well educated. She had an appreciation of art and fine things. She could ride...

She was almost tempted to tell him she was not totally working class, to say, Hey, half of me is Bingham blood. You know the Binghams, don't you? Smashing good family. They go back centuries. I don't know where they live, and they did give my mother the boot more than twenty-five years ago, but other than that I'm sure they're right up your alley!

'Uncle James doesn't like parties much,' Rebecca chimed in. 'Do you, Uncle James?'

'Not any more, sweetie.'

'Henry said you'd changed,' the child offered, giving additional information which had James's eyebrows lifting. 'He said you used to be a ''right royal raver'' in your younger days. But that nowadays you had ''settled down nicely''.'

Marina couldn't help a small laugh, for the child had imitated Henry's pompous manner to perfection.

'Henry said that to *you*?' James asked his niece in a disbelieving tone.

The child suddenly looked guilty. 'Well...um...no. Not exactly. He and William were having a cup of tea in the kitchen one day and I...I...'

'You eavesdropped,' James chided. 'You know that's not right, Rebecca.'

'I don't think it's so bad,' she defended herself. 'It's the only way I can find out interesting stuff. No one ever tells us kids anything!'

Marina struggled not to smile. And so did James, she saw. The corners of his mouth were definitely twitching. The car stopped at the front steps and Rebecca demanded to be let out immediately. William took too long to open doors these days, she confided to her uncle.

'All right, but don't run,' James warned, before he unzapped her seat belt and opened the car door. Rebecca jumped out and immediately raced up the front steps. Already a plump grey-haired lady was emerging from the house and holding her arms out to the child.

'That's Mildred,' he explained, sighing. 'She's been the housekeeper here for a hundred years. Or so it seems. She's actually only about sixty, and very attached to Rebecca. I don't know what she'll do if this transplant doesn't take. God, I don't know what *I'll* do, come to think of it,' he finished wretchedly.

Marina didn't stop to think. She simply reacted,

reaching out to touch his nearest arm. When he looked up at her with still sad eyes, she knew she would do anything to comfort him, regardless of the personal cost.

'You mustn't worry,' she said softly. 'And you mustn't fuss. Treat her like a normal child with a future. Have faith, James.'

'Faith?' He shook his head. 'I'm not a very religious person, I'm afraid.'

'What has that got to do with faith? Faith is simply believing. If you believe Rebecca will get better and you treat her as such, then *she* will believe she's going to get better and she will!'

He searched her eyes, with a type of wonder in his. 'Promise me you won't go back on tonight,' he suddenly urged in a low, husky voice. 'Promise me now. Say it!'

'I...I promise,' she whispered shakily.

'And not just for a short hour or two,' he insisted. 'All night.'

She shivered beneath the rather ruthless passion in his voice.

A nod was all she could manage this time.

William opened the passenger door at that precise moment, and Marina was relieved to turn away from James's disturbing intensity. But she knew it was only a temporary reprieve. Tonight she would place herself totally in his hands.

She hoped he would be merciful.

# CHAPTER ELEVEN

MARINA woke with a start, as you do when you have fallen asleep not in your own bed. She half sat up, glanced around the dimly lit room, then sank back down on top of the bed with a sigh, her eyes sliding across to the form sleeping beside her.

Rebecca looked totally at peace in sleep, as most children did. She'd hardly moved since she'd drifted off while Marina read to her, having worn herself out with showing her visitor absolutely everything on the estate. The house, the pool, the tennis court, the horses, the lake and the gazebo, chattering non-stop all the time.

When his niece had begun to droop after lunch, James had put his foot down and insisted she have a nap. Marina had lain down next to her on the bed to read her Enid Blyton's *The Magic Faraway Tree*, and in no time Rebecca had travelled from Faraway Land to the Land of Nod.

James had settled in an armchair across the room while this was going on, listening happily. When Rebecca had dropped off and Marina had tried to stop reading he'd insisted she go on. He'd wanted to hear the end of the story—claimed he'd adored Enid Blyton as a boy and could not get enough.

Marina could not recall if she'd finished the story.

At some stage she must have closed her eyes herself and nodded off. The book, she noted as she rolled over and peered down, was lying on the carpet. And James was...

Marina's head jerked up and she stared through the gloom, surprised to find James still there, his head sunk sidewards, fast asleep. Goodness, she thought. What on earth was the time?

She struggled to see her watch, surprised again to make out that it was not as late as the faded light indicated. Only six. It was then she noticed the drawn curtains. Had James done that? Or Mildred? Maybe Talbot, the butler?

She would not have put it past either of those last two, who were the nicest people. Mildred was a real sweetie and Talbot wasn't nearly as stuffy as Henry. There again, he was not of the old school. He was a very modern style of butler. In his late forties, fair, shortish but fit-looking, he was efficient, courteous and attentive without being obsequious or too pompous.

Although Marina had become perversely fond of Henry's old-fashioned ways, he could do with lightening up a bit, she believed.

Dinner was not to be served until seven-thirty, so Marina decided not to wake anyone else just yet. She was loath to disturb the soundly sleeping Rebecca, and there was something far too intimate about waking James from sleep for Marina's liking. With the evening at hand, she knew it was imperative for her to keep good control of her nerves—and the situation.

She'd got herself into a right state last night and she didn't want a repeat performance—certainly not until they were safely alone together.

Rebecca was an intuitive child, and for all her kindness Marina doubted Mildred had come down in the last shower. It seemed likely the housekeeper had turned a blind eye to many a liaison under this roof, if the previous Earl and his wife had been such a swinging jet-setting couple. The same went for Talbot. Butlers must surely notice things like that. But Marina didn't want any blind eyes being turned towards herself and the new Earl. She wanted the whole household to be genuinely blind to their relationship.

*Relationship?* sneered that rotten voice in her head. *What relationship? You're having a one-night stand with him, Marina, that's all. Don't go giving yourself airs and graces, now. You are not the love of His Lordship's life. You are a very convenient passing passion while Her Ladyship is making up her mind.*

'Oh, shut up!' she muttered under her breath, and swung her bare feet over the side of the bed. Pressing her lips firmly together, she slid her feet into her black flatties and stood to walk over to the nearest window, gripping the heavy green drapes and pulling them apart just enough to look down at the rolling hill and the lake.

The water looked beautiful in the late afternoon light. Like liquid glass.

Marina was thinking how magnificent it would look under moonlight when James suddenly materialised behind her, his hands curling over her shoulders.

When she went to whirl around, his grip tightened and he pulled her back against him.

'Don't,' she croaked.

He turned her round and looked deep into her shadowed eyes. 'Don't what?' he asked, his voice strained.

'Don't...do anything. Not here.' And she nodded over to the sleeping child on the bed.

His expression was pained. 'God, Marina, you frightened the life out of me there for a moment. I thought you were going to tell me tonight was off.'

'And if I did?' she whispered, in one last crisis of conscience.

'Then I would have to set out to change your mind back again,' he vowed fiercely. 'By fair means or foul.'

'You...you wouldn't do that,' she said shakily. 'You have too much honour.'

'This is beyond honour, Marina,' he said, with a dark and bitter resolve. 'Beyond anything I have ever known before. Believe me when I say if you don't come to my room later tonight, then, by God, I will come to yours!'

The image of his battering on her bedroom door in the middle of the night was nearly as appalling as her sneaking along to his.

'You won't have to do that,' she rasped. 'I...I'll come to your room. But only if you promise to do nothing to arouse anyone's suspicions during the course of the evening. Don't flirt with me, or...or look at me as you are doing at this moment.'

'When will you come?' he demanded to know.

'When the house is quiet and everyone has retired for the night. I don't want anyone to know, James. That's very important to me.'

'Fair enough. In that case, don't knock. I'll leave the door unlocked and the key on the inside. Simply slip in and turn the key. That should prevent any disaster such as Rebecca barging in in the middle of the night. Not that she's likely to do that. As you can see, she sleeps like a log.' And he nodded to the still unconscious child.

'Yes, but she may have had the edge taken off tonight's sleep with this nap.'

'She still wouldn't come to me if she woke. She'd ring for Mildred. Look, what say I suggest Mildred sleeps in the nanny's room tonight? It's right next to Rebecca's. Just in case Rebecca wakes and wants something.'

'Yes, yes, that would be good.' *Good?* Marina thought, appalled. *Good?* Nothing about this was good. It was underhanded and tawdry and just simply awful! She wanted to cry, to scream at him. *Beg* him not to do this to her—turn her into something she was not.

'Marina, don't worry so,' he chided, making everything so much worse with his own apparent ease. 'It's a very big house with very thick walls and doors. No one will know. I promise you. Now...' He reached out and touched her cheek, his fingertips like licks of flame against her skin. 'Do you know where my room is? We don't want you stumbling around the corridors, getting lost in the dark.'

'I won't get lost,' she said, jerking her face sharply so that his hand dropped away. 'I know exactly where your room is. Rebecca and Mildred gave me the grand tour of the house. Mildred was especially proud of the master of the house's bedroom.'

It was hardly just a room. It was a suite, with a separate sitting room, dressing room and bathroom, all sumptuously furnished. But of course it had been the huge bed which had drawn her eyes earlier that day. A four-poster, which Mildred informed her proudly had once belonged to one of the kings of France.

It was truly magnificent, with an elaborate carved bed-head and a solid rosewood canopy. But what had sent Marina's heart racing were the blue and gold brocade curtains sashed to each bedpost with gold tasselled cords, similar in style to those in her fantasy.

It was the most glorious bed Marina had ever seen. And the most seductive in her eyes. She'd had to work hard not to let her mind fill with new fantasies, all the more arousing because she knew this time she could make them come true, every single decadent one. She had thanked her lucky stars at the time that Rebecca had been showing her the house in Mildred's company, and not James's. If he'd been with them, she would surely have blushed furiously and perhaps made the housekeeper suspicious.

Even thinking about it brought a flushing heat to her face. James saw it, and enclosed her in his arms before she could think to struggle. 'Stop getting yourself all worked up,' he murmured as he moulded her body to his.

Her eyes rounded at the immediate wave of desire which swept through her body. It roared along her veins, curled through her stomach, then crashed against her thudding heart. A moan surfaced through an ebb tide of longing and starkly sexual need. He heard it and his arms tightened around her, making her hotly aware of his own need, which felt as intense as her own. But infinitely more powerful.

Panic-stricken, she pushed him away. Just in time, too. For there came a sound from the bed and she whirled to find Rebecca yawning and stretching. Marina could feel her cheeks burning but the child didn't seem to have overheard or seen anything.

'Was I asleep long?' Rebecca asked with a second yawn.

'Not too long,' Marina said lightly, and walked over to pick the book up from the floor. She didn't dare look back at James. 'But you'd better get up now. It's not that long till dinner.'

'Oh. I suppose we're having dinner in the dining room, are we, Uncle James?' She didn't sound at all thrilled with the idea.

'Yes,' he agreed. 'Why, would you prefer to eat with Mildred and Talbot in the kitchen?'

'Oh, yes, please. I hate sitting at that silly long table. I can never see anyone on the other side through the candles and flowers and stuff.'

James laughed and Marina's eyes snapped his way. He looked superbly in control, she realised. No one

would have guessed that a few moments ago he had
been so blatantly aroused.

'I can remember thinking exactly the same at your
age,' he tossed over his shoulder at Rebecca as he
strolled towards the door. 'Fair enough. I'll tell Talbot
it's just Marina and myself for dinner in the dining
room.'

'Am…am I supposed to get dressed up?' Marina
asked, before he could leave the room. Privately, she
was appalled at the prospect of having to sit in state
with James over a lengthy formal dinner, knowing
what was to come later.

He stopped with his hand on the door knob and
turned slowly to face her. His eyes were superbly
bland as they moved over her body. It was Marina
who was a shambles, her heart racing as his gaze
moved down over her breasts with their betrayingly
hard nipples poking through the soft wool.

'No,' he drawled. 'Wear what you've got on, if you
like. That looks lovely on you.'

His eyes returned to her face, where they remained
fixed for a fraction longer than necessary. And, in that
elongated and quite electric moment, she knew his
composure was just a façade. He was still as turned
on as she was. His need hadn't abated. Neither had
his passion. He was just better at hiding it than she
was, better at concealing his carnal desires behind a
cloak of restraint and respectability.

Marina felt anything but restrained and respectable
as she stared after his departing figure.

\*    \*    \*

By nine that evening Marina was almost beside herself with tension. Dinner was proving to be the trial she'd suspected it would be, despite the food being as superb as the setting.

She supposed most females would give their eye teeth to be wined and dined in such a room, with its walnut panelling and gracious antique furniture. Most females would probably give their eye teeth to be going to bed with the Lord of the Manor that night, whether he loved them or not!

But it seemed Marina was not most females. She kept wishing with all her heart that it was love stirring James to look at her as he was looking at her across the table, and not those infamous Winterborne hormones.

So much for her warnings about his staring at her with lustful eyes! It seemed she'd unleashed the beast in the Earl of Winterborne with her promise of things to come. He was making Shane look positively civilised with the way his glittering blue gaze kept fixing on her mouth and her breasts, not to mention their sinfully erect nipples!

By the time Rebecca was safely tucked up in bed around ten-thirty—the child had been quite lively after her afternoon nap, as predicted—and Marina could reasonably say her own goodnights just before eleven, she was a mess. She could also no longer delineate between nerves and desire. Her stomach churned. Her hands were clammy. Her body burned.

Once safely in her own lavish bedroom, she fairly dived into the gold-tapped *en suite* shower, staying there at length in an attempt to cool down her whole system while gathering some much needed composure.

But composure had apparently fled to the far corners of the earth. She groaned her dismay at her utter inner panic. Her mind spun with self-reproach.

Giving her so-called word like this was the worst and the stupidest thing she had ever done! My God, she'd promised to deliver herself to his bedroom like a…a…whore! In a way, she wished she *were* a whore, instead of the basically very inexperienced bedpartner she was. With Shane, she'd simply lain back and gasped in pleasure and surprise at what he'd done. Before Shane she hadn't done anything either, her two earlier boyfriends wanting nothing but quickies, she now realised. They hadn't required her to do anything except not stop them.

But James was a difficult kettle of fish. He would surely be expecting a woman of the world. Instead, he was going to get *her*!

Marina emerged from the shower, shaking.

As midnight drew near she knew she could not delay much longer. She was physically ready, her body washed and perfumed and naked beneath her nightwear. The oyster satin nightie and matching robe covering her nudity were very pretty, though not overly seductive. Oddly, she'd left her hair up, perhaps in defiance of her fantasy about her hair being spread out on a snow-white pillow.

Pride alone propelled her out of the room. No way

did she want James coming to her room and making a scene.

The walk down the corridors and along to James's wing did not take nearly long enough. Before she knew it she was standing at his door, and before she knew it he was sweeping that door open as though some sixth sense had told him she was there.

'Where in hell have you been?' he snapped, and, grabbing an arm, yanked her into the bedroom. Just as swiftly he shut and locked the door behind him.

There were no lights on in the room, she noted shakily, yet it wasn't in darkness. The curtains at the main windows were wide open and an eerie silver moonlight was streaming in, making the blues in the room look grey and the gold like platinum.

James was wearing a darkly patterned silk robe, tightly sashed around his waist as though he had sashed and resashed it many times in the last hour. His obvious agitation made her feel a little better. Clearly he wasn't in the habit of making midnight assignations with women he had not promised to love and cherish, but from whom he'd exacted a promise of total sexual surrender for one long, mad, marvellous night.

Suddenly it was all too much for her, and with a soft sound of just such sexual surrender she threw her arms around his neck and lifted her mouth for him to crush.

He crushed it at first. Then adored it, tasting her tongue and licking at her lips, making her mouth feel not so much a mouth but an exquisite meal, to be savoured before being devoured.

She was melting against him when his mouth turned savage again as abruptly as it had gentled, making her moan beneath its onslaught, half in fear, half with a wild, mutual passion.

He must have heard the fear, however, for he dragged his mouth away and buried it in her hair, his breath hot and ragged. 'You don't know what you do to me,' he rasped. 'I've been in hell all week. But this last hour has unravelled me completely. I'm not going to be able to last.'

His confessed vulnerability was oddly reassuring and sweetly touching. She pulled back to cup his face and look up at him.

'James,' she said softly, and traced over his face and mouth with gentle fingertips. 'Darling James...we have all night, remember? It doesn't matter.'

He groaned and opened his lips to take one of her fingertips between them. Desire flashed like lightning through her, and without thinking she pushed the finger further inside his mouth, watching with wide eyes and pounding heart while he sucked on it.

Marina had read about women going weak at the knees over a man but had thought it a melodramatic exaggeration.

But it wasn't. As he sucked her finger she literally went weak at the knees, her legs turning jelly-like. Her head began to whirl. She had to take her finger out or risk collapsing!

She plucked it away with a low moan of regret and

he just stared at her. Her hands moved as in a dream, slipping the robe from her shoulders to let it flutter to the floor. Then came the nightie, one strap at a time, till she was standing naked before him.

She had never felt so desirable in all her life. His hungry gaze gobbled her up, especially her breasts which already ached for his touch. She felt their aroused heaviness lift upwards when she raised her hands to pluck the pins from her hair. She dropped them on the carpet, one at a time, letting the mass of red-gold curls tumble around her bare shoulders in erotic disarray.

'I don't think one night is going to be enough,' he said thickly, and bent to scoop her up into his arms.

He carried her over and lay her down in the softest of mattresses and pillows. The blue and gold quilt was already thrown back, she realised as she sank into snow-white linen. Her hands lifted languidly again, to rake her hair out onto the pillow. If she was going to live out a fantasy, then she was going to do it right.

'Are you going to close the curtains?' she asked, her voice sounding as thick as treacle.

'And block out such a sight? God, no.' He began unsashing his own robe. 'Do you know what you look like lying there in the moonlight? Have you any idea?'

He shrugged out of his robe and Marina snapped out of her dreamworld. For never had she seen a man so fiercely erect. Not even Shane, who was a very virile fellow. James was awesome in his need. Like a volcano rising up and ready to explode.

The sight unnerved her momentarily.

'Don't…don't forget to use protection,' she said in a breathy little voice.

'I'm well prepared,' he assured her, and pointed to a pile of foil squares on the bedside table.

'Oh…'

He reached to pick one up and Marina turned her head away. She didn't want to watch.

But what if he asked *her* to put one on him later in the night? She turned her head back, only to find the deed already done.

Now she felt a fool. James's need for her wasn't embarrassing. It was beautiful. *He* was beautiful.

She held out her arms and he joined her on the bed, kissing her hungrily. Her own need, which had receded with their separation, quickly raced back. Soon she could not get enough of his tongue in her mouth, or that hand which was stroking up and down her leg. Gradually it moved higher, then around between her thighs. Once there, it did not hesitate. It was focused and experienced and merciless.

In no time Marina was on the brink, and she burst from his mouth, gasping. Her back began to arch away from the bed, her flesh tensing in readiness for that electric moment when everything twisted even tighter before splintering apart. He immediately moved between her legs and surged into her, deep and hard. She caught her breath, and tried to stop herself from coming. But such was the burst of emotional and physical satisfaction at being one with him at last that her body refused to obey.

She cried out, her face grimacing in that strange

agony which was really ecstasy. And then she felt *him* coming, shuddering violently into her. Her mind spun out into a vortex where all those tortuous feelings he'd been evoking in her since they'd met sought to find total satisfaction.

She found herself raking her nails down his back and digging them into the taut muscles of his buttocks. But if it was pain she was wanting to impart, then she failed. The only sound he made was a long, low groan of raw animal pleasure.

It did wicked things to her, that groan. She vowed to make him groan many times during the night; she vowed to make him suffer for doing this to her—for making her love him even more than she had before.

## CHAPTER TWELVE

'WHY is it,' James said softly, shortly before three, 'that the more I make love to you, the more I want to?'

He was lying on his side, propped up on his left elbow and trickling the tassel of one of the curtain cords over her nearest nipple.

Marina said nothing. She just clenched her jaw in futile denial of her own rapid resurgence of desire.

He started on the other nipple. 'You have such lovely breasts,' he murmured, and bent to lick the stiffened peak to an even greater state of acute sensitivity. After spending a full five minutes on this torture, he trailed the tassel down over her ribs and stomach, encircling her navel before moving down to her thighs, by which time Marina was breathing heavily and desperately wanting to part those thighs wide, to beg him to run that tantalising tassel over far more intimate places.

But a certain feminine stubbornness was creeping into Marina, an innate desire not to be so easy, she supposed. It was silly at this point, she knew, but she could not seem to help it. She kept her legs stubbornly closed, even when he drove her mad with that tassel trailing up and down her thighs.

Her resistance was perverse, really, because he'd

already kissed every inch of her, already reduced her several times to a quivering, mindless creature, unable to stop him doing whatever he pleased, wherever he pleased.

In the end, he stopped and frowned at her. 'What's wrong?' he asked.

'Nothing.'

'You don't want me to make love to you again?'

She said nothing. Wild horses were not going to drag the admission from her that she was dying for it already.

'Would you like to do it to me? Is that it?'

Her eyes blinked with the alien notion. For she had never ever made love to a man, not even Shane. He hadn't asked for it and she'd never offered, though she'd seen it often enough in the movies. It seemed the only position these days for sex scenes: the woman on top. To Marina it always looked choreographed, and frankly rather embarrassing.

'I...I've never done that sort of thing before,' she confessed.

His eyes showed surprise. 'Why's that?'

'I guess I...I never wanted to. And none of the men I've slept with have ever asked me to.'

'Not even Shane?'

'No.'

'I see. At least, no, I *don't* see. Damn it, Marina, must you confuse me even more than I am already?' He glared down at her with a mixture of exasperation and bewilderment. 'So tell me, exactly how many men have there been in your life so far?'

'Exactly how many women have there been in yours?'

The counter-question threw him. Clearly he could not even hazard a guess.

'Never mind,' she muttered. 'I get the point. I have technically had three lovers before you. But two of them were really just boys. I dated them at teachers' college. They were students, like me, with either limited experience or knowledge. I'm not sure which.'

She sighed at the memory. She'd been such a child at the time, yet thought herself so grown-up. All of eighteen and nineteen! 'I believed I was in love both times,' she said. 'But sex proved such an anticlimax on each occasion that I eventually decided what I felt couldn't possibly be love.

'That's why when sex with Shane was so unexpectedly good, I did the reverse and believed I *had* to be in love with him. Although, to be fair to myself, he was also very kind to me when I needed kindness. My mother had just died and I needed…someone.'

'I can understand that,' James murmured.

He idly resumed tantalising her with the tassel. Over her stomach this time. 'So you really haven't had all that much experience…?'

'No.' Her voice was as taut as her stomach muscles.

'That's a very exciting thought,' he said, trailing the tassel up over her breasts and up to her mouth, where he danced the ends of the golden threads over her softly quivering lips. 'Are you enjoying what I'm doing at the moment? You certainly seem to be.'

Her face flamed and she nodded, her tongue suddenly thick in her throat.

'If I asked you to, would you do it to me, Marina? Would you do all those things you have never done with a man before? You know what I mean, don't you?'

She nodded again, her heart pounding in her chest.

He stopped the torture with the tassel, and, taking her nearest hand, opened her clenched fingers and wrapped them tightly around the cord. Then he lay back on the bed beside her, his eyes shutting as he scooped in, then exhaled several very deep breaths.

Her stomach churned as she propped herself up on one arm and stared, first down at the cord in her hand, then over at his outstretched nakedness. She wanted to. Oh, yes. She wanted to touch him and kiss him all over, to trail the tassel over *his* flesh till he was groaning with passion. She wanted to make love to him better than all those other women, the ones he could not count.

But she had no experience to fall back on, and her mouth went dry at the prospect at making an utter fool of herself.

'You don't have to do anything you're not comfortable with,' he reassured her softly, even while his eyes remained shut. 'I'll love anything you do to me. Anything at all.'

Marina gathered all her courage and just began, her hand trembling. His chest quivered at the first touch of the soft golden threads, his lungs expanding on an inward gasp of pleasure. She took confidence from the sound and started trailing the tassel over his broadly muscled male chest. He sucked in sharply again when she grazed over his nipples.

So she did it again. Then again, thrilling to the sight of those small nubs expanding into twin peaks of expectant nerve-endings. Marina knew how they felt, for she had felt the same thing herself. With the knowledge of her own experience in mind, she bent over him and used her tongue on them in long, teasing licks, and eventually he gave out a muffled groan, the sound vibrating with tortured arousal.

A bolt of adrenaline raced through her as she discarded the cord and moved her mouth and hands slowly downwards, over his ribs and onto his stomach. When she swirled her tonguetip in his navel, his stomach fluttered wildly. When she moved on even further, she felt every muscle in his body freeze in anticipation of what was to come.

She didn't dare look up to see if he'd opened his eyes. If she did, this new and intoxicating boldness might fail her. As it was, she felt dizzy with an unexpected sense of power, and possessed by the most incredible passion. She'd never realised how exciting taking control of lovemaking could be, how much she would revel in the feel of his hardness beneath her hands and within her mouth.

'Don't stop,' he rasped when her head finally lifted. 'For pity's sake, don't stop.'

It still seemed the ideal time to do so, and to reach for one of the foil packets. He groaned and grimaced, his whole body as tightly strung as his face. She took

her time, partly because she'd never actually put a
condom on before but mostly because underneath her
seeming cool she was so hopelessly excited she
couldn't think straight.

'God, yes,' he cried, when she finally moved to
straddle him. When she began lowering herself rather
gingerly onto his powerful erection, he took hold of
her hips and pulled her down onto him more quickly.

Marina gasped at the feel of his flesh impaling hers,
her mouth drying as her lips parted and hot, shallow
breaths puffed from her panting lungs.

He reached up to knead her swollen breasts, crushing them together then drawing them down, down to
his mouth. She bent forward in a type of daze, only
dimly aware that she was no longer in control. *He*
was.

He was suckling on her breasts and she was moaning, moaning and moving her bottom, writhing in her
need. His own buttocks were rocking against the bed,
setting up a frantic rhythm inside her. With a tortured
gasp, she plucked her nipple out of his mouth and
straightened so that she could match his movements
with more uninhibited fervour. She no longer thought
such an act embarrassing, or ridiculous. She no longer
thought at all.

They came together like a thunderclap, and their
cries echoed through the room. Afterwards she col-
lapsed upon his chest, utterly spent. James clasped her
close and buried his lips in her hair.

'God, how am I going to live without you?'
he muttered.

The very real bleakness in his voice stirred Marina to hope as she had never hoped this past week. She waited breathlessly for him to say he loved her, to ask her to stay in England with him. But he remained silent. Clearly, no matter what his feelings for her, they were not strong enough, or deep enough, for him to change the path of his life.

Marina had not really expected him to. Men like him did not marry girls like her. A soul-sinking acceptance of the situation combined with her physical exhaustion, and she sighed a deep yawn.

'Don't go to sleep, for pity's sake,' he groaned. 'The morning will come soon enough.'

'It's almost morning now,' she told him drowsily.

'We still have a couple of hours. Talk to me,' he urged as he held her and stroked her spine. 'Tell me all about yourself. Tell me about your childhood, your teaching. Tell me what you do in a typical day. I want to know everything about you, Marina.'

It seemed pointless, but she did as he asked and told him of her upbringing, her school days, her wish to become a teacher—but not in her mother's riding school. She told him of her college years and how, after her unsatisfactory relationships with the opposite sex, she'd steered clear of boyfriends for a few years and filled her life with her career.

And as she talked that crushing exhaustion gradually left her. Just before the dawn it was James who fell asleep, leaving Marina to disentangle herself from his leaden arms. She crept back to her room, where she sat in an armchair and watched the sun rise. She dozed in the chair for an hour or so, waking when the mantel clock donged seven. With a sigh she rose and made her way to the shower, wondering as she stepped under the jets of hot water if James was still asleep.

She rather resented washing the smell of him from her. Making love with this man who she knew she *really* loved had been the most incredible experience she had ever had. She would never forget it. Neither would she regret it.

To know true love was a rare thing, she believed. That was why it had been impossible for her to turn her back on it entirely, to not grab the one opportunity she was given to consummate her feelings, even if having that one incredible night with him made her grieve over all the coming nights—and years—when she would never know his touch again.

Marina felt the tears come then. She lifted her face and let the water wash them away before she ended up with great puffy red eyes. There were too many intuitive people around Winterborne Hall for her to go down to breakfast looking as if she'd been crying.

It was while she was under the shower and had moved on to shampooing her hair that Marina suddenly remembered her hairpins, scattered all over the floor by the bed in James's bedroom.

She didn't know what to do. James was certain not to see them. Men like him, who had nothing to do with housework, would never notice a few hairpins lying on the carpet. But a housemaid would. And so would Mildred. They were very distinctive-looking pins, especially made for putting up long hair. Two and two would soon make four in the mind of who-ever found them.

Marina knew she could not bear to go through this day fearing she was being looked at, and sniggered over, and pitied.

She had no alternative but to go and get them.

She dressed quickly, in the jeans and white shirt she'd worn over on the plane. She hadn't come with a whole swag of clothes for cooler weather and had little choice.

It was just going on eight by the time she was ready for her rescue mission. Drying her hair had taken some time, but she didn't want to waltz around the house at this hour with dripping locks. It would look suspicious. This way, if she ran into anyone in the hallways, she could say she was an early riser and was going for a walk.

Unfortunately James's room was not situated be-tween her room and the staircase which led down-stairs. Hopefully, being Sunday morning, not too many people would be up and about yet. She wasn't expected down to breakfast till nine, James having made this arrangement with Talbot over dinner the night before.

Rebecca was a worry. Children were notorious early risers. Then there was Mildred, who no doubt was of the old school who got up at the crack of dawn. Still, the housekeeper was more likely to already be downstairs. Or in church, with a bit of luck.

A peep out of the bedroom door showed an empty

hallway. Marina scooped in one last steadying breath, then made a determined dash in the direction of James's room, hurrying along the wide polished and carpeted corridors, not stopping on the way to admire any of the gilt-framed portraits and landscapes as she'd done during her tour the previous day.

Once in front of James's solid wooden door she knocked, before fear and panic got the better of her.

When Talbot opened the door, she almost died.

'Yes, miss?' he said, without turning a hair, as though it was perfectly normal for breathless ladies to call upon the Lord of the Manor at eight in the morning.

'I...er...I was hoping to have a brief word with James. Is he...er...in?'

'His Lordship is in the shower. Can I help you with anything, perhaps?'

'No. No, I don't think so.' She glanced past the butler and into the room, trying to see if the pins were still on the floor. The bed, she could see with a sinking heart, was already made. A tray with a silver coffee service and a newspaper was on the bedside table nearest the door—the same bedside table which the night before had held much more intimate items. 'Er...what time did James say breakfast was last night?'

'Nine, miss.' The butler frowned ever so slightly, then gave a small knowing nod, rather reminiscent of Henry's body language. 'Just one moment, miss,' he said, and disappeared for a few seconds before reappearing and holding out his hand. 'I think, perhaps, these are yours.'

She took the hairpins and wished with all her heart that the polished wooden floor would open up and swallow her.

'I won't mention finding them to His Lordship, miss,' Talbot added, without a hint of conspiracy and totally ignoring her wild blush. 'Or your little visit here this morning. It would only upset him.'

Marina was taken aback. She blinked, then glared at the butler through her own distress.

*Well, we wouldn't want that, would we?* scorned that brutally honest side of hers, which responded rather badly to hypocrisy and double standards. *To hell with your feelings, Miss Marina, as long as we don't upset His Lordship!*

'Thanks a million,' she snapped, and, whirling, she stalked off, the pins clenched in an angry fist.

What a first-class idiot she was to ever hope that what they'd shared last night might mean something special to James! Okay, so he might not love her as she loved him, but it was galling to find out she was probably one in a long line of ladies who'd left pins behind in his bedroom. Or panties. Or whole damned negligées!

As for Talbot—there were no flies on *him*! Clearly James had trained him better than Henry! Talbot probably had a whole cupboard full of ladies' leftovers somewhere! No doubt he'd even prepared the room for His Lordship last night beforehand, delicately leaving behind a ready supply of condoms in case His Lordship had an unfortunate slip of memory.

Can't have the Winterborne blood being contaminated in any way, can we? Can't go letting *common* flesh get too close to the purer strains. After all, commoners might have unspeakable diseases. Or, worse, they might actually *breed*!

Marina had worked herself up to a good head of steam by breakfast time. But once Rebecca joined her on the stairs, holding her hand and chattering away like the happy little girl she was, Marina resolved to put her bad temper aside. What would be the point in spoiling the day for Rebecca by being cranky? Or in spoiling the day for herself? She'd known the score, hadn't she?

But it was infinitely hard to hold her tongue when James came downstairs in a darkly brooding mood. He presented himself briefly in the morning room, saying he wouldn't be having any breakfast and that he'd already had coffee in his room. He then disappeared into his study with the excuse that he had estate business to attend to while he was down.

A most put-out Marina was left to entertain Rebecca, who didn't seem to mind. If Marina hadn't liked the child so much she might have gone and given James a piece of her mind. How dared he treat her so shabbily? As it was, she set to giving the little girl some quality time while they could be together. After all, Rebecca had to go back to the hospital that afternoon.

'I don't want you to ever go back home, Marina,'

the child said with touching sincerity, over the morning tea party they were having in the gazebo. 'Can't you stay longer?'

'I'm afraid not, sweetie. I really must be going home. Oh, dear!' she exclaimed as a thought struck.

'What is it?'

'I just realised. I…I haven't rung home to let them know I'm catching the next plane. I wonder what time it is in Sydney? I think there's ten hours' difference, which would make it nine at night. I'll have to go back to the house and ring straight away, Rebecca. You'd best come with me.'

'Oh, do I have to?'

Marina had no intention of leaving the seven-year-old unattended next to a lake. 'Yes, you do,' she insisted. 'It'll only be for a few minutes. Come on.'

'Oh, all right. I'll go and talk to Mildred.'

Mildred directed Marina to James's study door, then walked off with her charge already talking fifty to the dozen. Marina knocked, and entered after a brusque, 'Come in.'

James was indeed sitting behind a desk. But he wasn't working. He was leaning back in a large wing-backed leather chair and seemed to be contemplating his shoes, which were propped up on the leather-topped desk.

He's been avoiding me, Marina realised.

His feet dropped to the floor at her entrance, but that wasn't as far as her heart had dropped. He snapped forward, clearly agitated by her sudden appearance. 'I thought you were Talbot,' he said.

'No, it's just me,' she retorted coldly. 'Last night's lay.'

His eyes showed shock at her words. *And* her tone.

'I have to ring Sydney,' she went on curtly. 'I need to tell Shane to meet the following day's plane. Mildred said I could use the phone in the hall, but I'm funny about things like using other people's phones for long-distance calls. I worry about the money it's costing.

'Silly me!' She smirked at his still shocked face. 'I should have realised money means nothing to men like you. Sorry for interrupting your work. I'll just trundle on back the way I came and use the phone in the lower hallway, like Mildred said.

'Don't worry. I'll soon get the hang of doing in Rome as the Romans do. It's just that I'm not used to creeping into a gentleman's bedroom in the dead of night. I'm not used to a gentleman's gentleman secretly handing me my hairpins in the morning like it was the most normal thing in the world. And I'm certainly not used to my lovers—as pathetically few as they have been—treating me the next morning like I have a contagious disease. As I said. Silly me!'

She spun on her heels to leave, and would have done so if he hadn't grabbed her from behind, pulling her back against him and kicking the door shut with his foot. With an amazing burst of strength she wrenched out of his hold and whirled, her hand slicing across his face with incredible force. The sound of it striking his cheek was like the crack of a bull whip.

She stared, stunned, as the perfect imprint of her hand flared against his skin.

'Oh!' she cried, then stared down at her own stinging hand. She might have burst into tears if she hadn't been so appalled.

James just stood there, his hand lifting slowly to trace the red welts as they rose. 'Remind me not to grab you too often,' he said drily.

'James, I'm sorry!' she blurted out.

'Don't be,' he said. 'I dare say I deserved it. And it's I who am sorry. I didn't stop to think how my mood this morning might appear to you. Lords don't often have to think of others, although I honestly do try to.'

Which he did, she knew. She'd seen the evidence of his thoughtfulness. With William. And Henry. And Rebecca.

'You can make your call in here,' he said, and pointed to the phone on the desk. 'I think I'd best go and put a cold compress on this.'

Marina groaned once he'd left the room. She felt bitterly ashamed of herself. He hadn't made false promises to her. He hadn't treated her that badly. She'd had no right to hit him. She was acting like a melodramatic fool!

Sighing, she walked slowly over to pick up the receiver, having to stop and think at length before remembering the overseas codes and dialling.

Shane answered fairly quickly.

'Yep?' he said succinctly.

'Shane, it's Marina.'

'About time, too, madam. I was beginning to think you'd forgotten me.'

'Of course I haven't forgotten you,' she said carefully. She had no intention of breaking up with him over the phone and thousands of miles away. To do so would be cruel, and Shane didn't deserve that. 'The thing is, Shane, today's plane was overbooked and they've asked me to delay my flight till tomorrow.'

'What? With a first-class seat? You just damned well tell them that's not on. Insist on the Sunday flight.'

Marina sighed. 'I can't do that, Shane.'

'Women!' he scorned. 'How do you ever think you're going to get on in this world if you don't insist on your rights? Your mother would have told them what for, Marina. She was one tough lady. Still, I guess the airline pays for everything when this happens, don't they? But don't let them put you in some second-class joint tonight. Insist on a five-star hotel, with taxis to and fro.'

'I'm staying the extra night at His Lordship's apartment in London,' she explained. 'It's in Mayfair. And his car will take me to the airport.'

'My, my, how toffy! So what's the old geezer like, eh?'

The old geezer walked in at that point and stood there, watching her. Marina was somewhat relieved to see his cheek had returned to normal.

'He's very nice,' she murmured.

'And very rich.' Shane sounded envious. 'Has he

given you a gift in appreciation of your generosity in going over there?'

'Not exactly.'

'What do you mean by not exactly?'

'Well, he *has* put all he owns at my disposal,' she said, her chin lifting as their eyes met across the room. 'And that's been very…memorable.'

'Pigs! The least he could have done was give you something personal.'

'I must go, Shane. This is costing a fortune. Don't forget to meet the plane.'

'See yuh.'

She hung up and battled to stop her chin from quivering.

'You're not still going to marry him, are you?' James asked in a disbelieving voice.

She laughed the threatened tears away. But it was not a nice laugh. ''You're not still going to marry Lady Tiffany, are you?'' she shot straight back.

'But you don't *love* him,' he went on, as if he hadn't heard her counter-argument.

'And you don't love *her*!' she cried, and threw her arms up in the air at his obtuseness. 'For pity's sake, face it, James. Whether you love *me* or not is immaterial. You don't love *her*. If you did, you would have made love to her by now. Nothing would have stopped you. Not honour, conscience or some stupid sacred duty to her brother!

'You're a passionate man. For you, love and sex will never be separated. You might like and admire her. You might feel responsible for her. You might

wish to protect and cherish her. But you absolutely
do not love—'

A loud 'ahem' in the open doorway behind James
stopped Marina in her tracks. It was the inimitable
Talbot, doing a perfect imitation of Henry at his most
formal.

'I'm sorry to interrupt, My Lord. But you have a
visitor.'

James turned slowly. Stiffly. 'A visitor?'

'Yes, My Lord. Lady Tiffany.'

Marina threw a shocked James an equally shocked
look.

'Lady Tiffany?' he echoed, his voice taut.

'Yes, My Lord. She's waiting for you in the drawing room. She wishes to see you…alone.'

There was a moment's fraught silence.

'Please tell Lady Tiffany that I will be along
shortly.'

'Yes, My Lord.' The butler gave the minutest of
bows and was gone.

Marina had to admire the swift way James had
composed himself. But what on earth was Tiffany doing back in England a day earlier than expected? And
why had she hot-footed it straight down *here*?

Her actions smacked of something suspicious.
Marina wondered now if she had been told something
about herself and James. Had there been some gossip
which had led to that phone call on Friday about her
having second thoughts?

Marina recalled the media had snapped more than
a few shots of her and James together the Wednesday

he'd brought her home from the hospital, one with his arm around her waist. It had been in all the morning papers. Maybe someone had also seen them together at the theatre and had hurried to inform Tiffany. People could be dreadful mischief-makers.

Another more horrible thought intruded.

'James, surely Henry would not have—?'

'No,' he broke in curtly. 'Henry would *not* have.' He came forward and took her by the shoulders, holding her firmly and forcing her to look him square in the eye. 'Before I see what Tiffany wants,' he ground out, 'tell me one thing. What was behind your tirade a minute ago? Dare I hope you really, truly love me, Marina? Or was there some other reason for it?'

'I...I...'

'Don't lie to me. I need to know the truth.'

Hope filled her heart at his passionately urgent demand. 'Yes,' she told him. 'Yes, I do love you. Really. Truly.'

'Dear God, why didn't you say so last night?'

'Why didn't *I*? Why didn't *you*?'

He looked bewildered. 'How could I, when I thought you were leaving me to go back to Australia, that all I could have with you was just the one night?'

Her breath caught. 'I...I only said that because I was so sure you didn't really love me, that all you wanted was sex.'

'Ahh.' He sighed deeply, then smiled the widest, most satisfied smile. 'Stay here, my love. I'll try not to be too long.'

Marina watched him stride out of the room, her heart already racing along with her mind.

His love...

He'd called her his love.

He loved her. He really, truly loved her—loved her more than he'd ever loved Tiffany.

Armed with that knowledge, Marina knew she would go to the ends of the earth for him now. He would never have to live without her. Never, for as long as they lived!

# CHAPTER THIRTEEN

MARINA was pacing impatiently around the room when Talbot appeared in the doorway.

'His Lordship would like you to join him and Lady Tiffany in the drawing room, miss,' the butler announced. 'It's the second door along on your—'

'Yes, yes, Talbot,' she broke in agitatedly. 'I know where it is. Thank you.'

Talbot disappeared and Marina sucked in several steadying breaths. But to no avail. She was suddenly besieged by nerves, and the most undermining thoughts.

Why hadn't James come back to get her himself? Had Tiffany dashed straight home from Italy after the wedding because she regretted her phone call the other day? Was she at this very moment begging James's forgiveness, telling him she loved him and still wanted to marry him? Had he taken one look at her perfectly matched self and decided he could not possibly throw away the life he had planned with her in favour of a working-class Aussie girl he'd only just met?

Marina knew she was being ridiculously negative, but it was still with great reluctance that she stepped out into the hallway and headed towards the drawing room.

During her grand tour the previous day, Marina had thought the drawing room the most welcoming room in the house. The wallpaper was a soft green, with white flowers strewn across it. The drapes at the tall windows were gold and the carpet a toning pattern. The furniture, which was arranged in cosy groups, consisted of armchairs covered in green and gold brocade and various mahogany side-tables on which sat vases of fresh flowers picked from the gardens.

The whole room had a warm and friendly look.

But Marina felt anything but warm at that moment. Her stomach churned as she reached the drawing room doorway, then contracted at the sight before her eyes. James was standing in front of the fireplace, his arms around Tiffany. She had her head on his chest and she was weeping. Was that good news or bad?

'Don't cry, Tiffany, love,' James was saying in soothing tones. 'There's no reason to cry now, is there? You've done nothing to be ashamed of or feel guilty over. You're one of the sweetest, nicest girls I've ever known. And I still love you dearly. Don't distress yourself so. This is not the end of the world.'

Marina must have made some sound, for James glanced up and smiled an apologetic smile at her.

'Sorry to send Talbot for you,' he told her gently, 'but Tiffany was upset, as you can see. Though not about what you might be thinking,' he added. 'I haven't had the opportunity to explain about us. Tiffany has been telling me about this man she met in Italy. And fell in love with...'

Marina's eyebrows shot up as her heart leapt with a combination of shock and delight.

Lady Tiffany, who was looking beautiful and fragile in a pale blue dress, drew back from James's arms and shot Marina a confused look. 'Us?' she repeated, glancing from Marina back to James.

'Yes, Tiffany, *us*,' he confessed firmly. 'Marina and myself. Come over here, darling,' he said, and stretched out a beckoning arm towards her.

Marina's insides were trembling as she walked into its welcoming warmth, all her nerves and doubts disappearing as James gathered her to his side.

'We fell in love with each other this past week,' he told Tiffany gently. 'We didn't mean for it to happen any more than you meant to fall in love with your Italian. We tried to fight our feelings, but in the end fate conspired against us and we... Well I have to confess that our relationship has progressed beyond the platonic.'

Tiffany was definitely looking a little shell-shocked, but not at all shattered.

'But I want you to know,' Marina added, 'that till you rang James on Friday he was a perfect gentleman—and fiancé—in every way.'

'I'm quite sure he was,' Tiffany agreed sincerely, then smiled up at him. 'Oh, James, this is such wonderful news. You've made me feel so much better! There I was, terrified that along with losing your good opinion of me I might have broken your heart. But I can see that it is in very safe hands indeed. I could not hope for you to find someone any sweeter than

Marina, here.' And she came forward and kissed Marina on the cheek.

'And what a lucky girl you are too, Marina,' Tiffany continued. 'To have a man like James fall in love with you. I admire him more than any man I know. To be honest, I have hero-worshipped him since I was a little girl.'

'Come now, Tiffany,' James muttered. 'Don't go embarrassing me.'

'What is embarrassing about my saying I have always loved you? For I have. And I still do. But I see now it is not the sort of love a wife should have for her husband. Just as the love you have for me is not the sort of love a husband should have for a wife.'

'Tiffany, I—'

'No, no, James, let me finish. I think Marina should hear this too.'

Marina was all ears. She had never heard anything she wanted to hear more.

'I know about the solemn promise you made to Peter, how you vowed to look after me if ever anything happened to him. That was why you asked me to marry you in the first place, wasn't it? Because you thought I needed you by my side to protect me from this world. And I can understand why. I have been such a child. About everything. But I think I'm on the way to growing up a bit now.

'My Italian taught me in a single hour what twenty-one years of being the naive child of my hopelessly old-fashioned and starchily staid parents could never teach me. What true love was all about. What desire was. And passion!'

'Tiffany!' James exclaimed, shock in his voice. 'You haven't? You didn't? Not after one miserable hour with a man you'd just met?'

'Oh, dearest James, of course not. I couldn't change the habits of a lifetime that quickly. But I wanted to. Oh, how I wanted to. You and Marina must know what that is like, being in love yourselves.'

James was not going to be so easily mollified. Clearly he was also not about to forget that promise to Tiffany's brother. 'That's all very well, but who *is* this man? Where did you meet him? Does he love you back?'

Tiffany's smile made her whole face light up. 'He said he did. A hundred times. Oh, James, he is so wonderful. And so handsome. And so...so...'

'Sexy?' Marina inserted mischievously.

Tiffany's high colour and slightly flustered state transformed her from her usual cool beauty to a creature of startling sensuality. Her Italian lover might not yet have taken her virginity, but he'd certainly given her innocence a nudge.

'Yes, *very* sexy,' she admitted, and blushed even more furiously.

'But can he look after you?' James demanded to know. 'Has he a job? He doesn't know you're from a titled family, does he?'

Marina could only smile at this very male trait of looking first to financial matters. But she was glad James didn't seem to notice the change in the girl. He must truly love *her* not to be affected by Tiffany's blossoming sexuality.

'James, don't badger the girl!' Marina protested. 'When are you going to see your Italian again, Tiffany?'

'He'll be in London next week,' she said excitedly. 'His family are in fashion. The Ferruccis. You must have heard of them. They own an exclusive label, with boutiques all over the world, so I don't think you have to worry about Marco being a gold-digger, James, dear.

'Besides, we Ravensbrooks don't have that much money left anyway. My father's already frittered away most of the family's fortunes. Why do you think I have a job as a tour guide over at Bellham Castle? Any man marrying me certainly won't be marrying me for my money!'

James frowned. 'He's asked you to marry him already?'

'No, of course not. But he will,' she said, with all the confidence of the young and inexperienced.

Marina was not about to disillusion her by saying that men didn't always ask the girls they said they loved to marry them. They *made* love to them. But that was a different matter entirely.

Marina's thoughts suddenly struck closer to home. James claimed he loved her—and she really didn't doubt that—but his claim hadn't been accompanied by an offer of marriage. Of course he'd hardly had the opportunity, but maybe he never would. Maybe his loving her was not going to be enough to take them to the altar together. Not in *his* world.

A knot of immediate tension formed in Marina's stomach. Was it all too good to be true?

Tiffany stayed a little while longer, chattering away about her gorgeous Italian, who had been a guest at one of the pre-wedding parties and then at the wedding itself, where he hadn't minded her purple bridesmaid dress at all. Probably because his family's bridal boutique in Rome had provided all the clothes for the wedding party.

He wasn't a relative of the bride and groom. Or a personal friend. In fact the bride and groom hadn't been aware of his true identity. To them he'd been merely the man from the bridal boutique who was contacted when one of the dresses hadn't shown up.

The bride's mother had been so impressed with his helpfulness and charm that she had impulsively invited him to both the pre-wedding party that night and the wedding itself. It was Tiffany who was to later find out he was one of the famed Ferruccis, although he had modestly declined her wish to tell all and sundry. He'd said he was enjoying being treated like a nobody.

'I have heard the name Ferrucci,' James said, still not sounding happy. 'But I know nothing of the family. I'm also not sure your folks will be happy with your getting mixed up with some Italian, Tiffany.'

'They'll have to like it or lump it, I'm afraid. I'll be twenty-one next month. I think that's old enough to make my own decisions, don't you?'

Personally, Marina thought twenty-one was still awfully young. She'd been a right ninny at twenty-one.

*And you're still a ninny,* that perverse voice piped up. *Thinking that the Earl of Winterborne was going to marry you!*

'I'd better be going,' Tiffany said. 'But before I do I want to tell you how happy I am for you both. I think you're much better suited to James than me, Marina. You'll be able to stand up to him. And you're nice and tall as well. James always rather overawed me a bit.'

'And your Italian doesn't overawe you?' James asked.

Tiffany's laugh was a little self-conscious. 'Oh, yes, he does. Terribly. But in a different and rather delicious way. It...it's hard to explain,'

Marina knew exactly what Tiffany meant.

'You be careful with this Italian fellow, Tiffany,' James warned. 'Don't rush into things. Men of his ilk are used to girls coming across without their having to promise them anything.'

'Oh, Marco's not like that,' Tiffany denied. 'He's very passionate, but very sincere. He said he's prepared to wait for me for for ever, if necessary. But I don't think he'll have to wait as long as that.' And she winked at them both.

When James scowled, Tiffany laughed. 'Do stop worrying, James. I promise I won't do anything *you* wouldn't do with Marina. Now I simply must go. Walk me to the car, will you?'

They did, and waved her off. But once the car was out of sight Marina turned to him and voiced the mounting worry in her mind.

'Interesting observation about the male gender you made just then,' she began, matter-of-factly, even though she felt nauseous inside. 'So tell me—are you going to prove to be a man of that ilk you spoke of, who expects a girl to come across without him promising her anything? Is your so-called love for me just words, or are you going to put a decent proposal where your mouth is?'

'Ahh,' he said. 'Trust you to cut straight to the crux of the matter.'

'It's the nature of the beast,' she agreed, rather tartly. 'Well, James? Are you going to ask me to marry you or not? Because if you're not, then don't expect a repeat performance of last night. For all his miserliness, Shane at least gave me an engagement ring in exchange for my favours in bed!'

James glared at her for a moment, then took her arm and started propelling her down the front steps.

'What? Where are you taking me? Take your hands off me and just answer the question, damn you!'

'I will, when I'm good and ready,' he said curtly. 'Now, do please shut that very loud mouth of yours for a few miserable seconds, will you? I do not want William, who is just over there washing the car, knowing my private business.'

'No kidding?' she mocked. 'Since when do the aristocracy care about their staff knowing their private business? Talbot already knows exactly what went on in your room last night, and I'll warrant William has a pretty good idea too!'

'Be quiet, woman, or by God I'll make more noise than you—and in a way that will have William and the rest of the household scandalised for a decade!'

'Why, you're nothing but a bully!' she protested as he shepherded her across the lawn and down to the boatshed on the edge of the lake. Once there, he wrapped a solid arm around her waist, opened the door, hoisted her off her feet and carried her inside, then kicked the door shut behind him.

'Tiffany was right to dump you,' she huffed and puffed. 'Keep this manhandling stuff up and I'll dump you as well.'

'The only one being dumped around here is *you*, Miss Loud Mouth.' And he dropped her onto an old divan in the corner.

She stared up at him as he stripped his sweater over his head and tossed it aside, then began with breathless speed on his trousers. 'You wouldn't!' she gasped, despite her eyes being glued to his body and her pulse-rate accelerating like mad.

'I surely would. So get your gear off as well, my dear future wife.'

'Your what?'

'You heard what I said.'

'Oh!' she cried. 'You mean it? You really mean it?'

'Is this the body of a man who doesn't mean what he says?'

'I mean about us getting married, silly.'

'Of course I mean it. Would a peer of the realm lie to you?' He bent and began attacking the buttons of her shirt. Marina immediately found it hard to concentrate on anything but James's busy fingers, which were unhooking her bra in no time flat.

'Are you saying lords don't lie?' she asked, rather breathlessly.

'Not *this* lord.' The bra gone, he tipped her backwards again and started on the jeans.

'I...I didn't think lords married girls like me.'

He laughed. 'Wherever did you get such a crazy idea? Lords have been known to marry girls a lot more unsuitable than you, my darling Marina. At the turn of the century they went through a phase of marrying chorus girls and actresses—which, believe me, at that time were one rung above a woman of the streets. And then there was my own brother,' James went on as Marina's jeans joined the rest of her clothes. 'He married one of the notorious Bingham girls.'

Marina's head jerked up to stare at him. 'B-Bingham girls?' she croaked.

James took no notice of her horrified expression, his eyes focused on divesting her of her white lace panties while he raved on. 'I suppose you haven't heard of the Binghams all the way over in Australia?

'Their father was Sir Richard Bingham, knighted for his dubious contributions to trade and industry. An ambitious rogue if ever there was one. Still, he was filthy rich and spoiled his daughters rotten. A wild lot, the four of them, with little reputation left by the time they reached puberty. But damned beautiful. I'll give them that. All of them with names beginning with J.

'Joy, my brother's wife, was the youngest—though she was, in fact, a good few years older than Laurence. She had a twin sister who ran off with some stablehand barely a week before she was to marry some aging Italian count. Can't think what her name was. Jasmine? No, that was the eldest. And Janet was the middle girl. Oh, yes. It was Jocelyn.'

Marina gasped.

James pulled her up to his chest, their bodies already fused. 'Yes, I know,' he rasped. 'You take my breath away too. God, I've been thinking of nothing else but this since I woke this morning. Why do you think I was in such a black mood? And why do you think I avoided you like poison? One look at you and I was in agony. On top of that, I thought you were going to leave me and go back to Australia and marry that Shane person.'

'Never,' she choked out, her head whirling.

'We're going to have to get married soon, darling. I can't keep dragging you into boatsheds at inappropriate times. No, don't move. I can't bear it when you move. Oh, God, Marina. Yes, all right, move. Oh, my darling...my darling...'

# CHAPTER FOURTEEN

'YOU'RE very quiet,' James said.

They were on their way back to London. William was busy negotiating the Sunday afternoon traffic, bumper to bumper in parts, and Rebecca was sound asleep again, with her head on a cushion in Marina's lap.

'Are you having second thoughts about my proposal?' he asked quietly.

'Are *you*?' she countered.

'Not at all. And if you're worried about being accepted as my wife then don't be. As I said before, that kind of snobbery is dead and gone. You saw the way Mildred reacted when I told her. She was very pleased. And Talbot, I assure you, was more than pleased when I told him. He said you were a lovely lady and wished us every happiness.'

'That's all very well, but what about Henry? I don't think Henry's going to be at *all* pleased.'

'Henry will get used to the idea.'

'Never in a million years. He had your life all mapped out, as the best Earl of Winterborne for a hundred years along with the perfect wife by your side. And it wasn't me,' she finished unhappily.

'I don't think you know Henry as well as you think you do. One of the reasons he was all for Tiffany was because Rebecca liked her so much. Once he realises Rebecca's as crazy about you as I am, then you will have a new champion, I assure you.

'Frankly, I suspect you've already won the old coot over. I recognised the signs all last week. It was just his loyalty and liking for Tiffany that was getting in the way. After I explain Tiffany's change of heart, he'll feel free to grovel at your feet as I'm sure he would like to.'

'Henry, grovel?' Marina exclaimed, though somewhat soothed and flattered by James's assertions. 'Henry would never grovel.'

'Smiling is Henry's way of grovelling. Once he starts smiling at you, you're in.'

'He *did* almost smile at me once,' Marina remarked thoughtfully.

James bestowed a real smile on her. 'See? What did I tell you? You have nothing to worry about.'

Except that I haven't told you yet I'm one of those notorious Bingham girls, Marina thought ruefully.

Rebecca was teary at the hospital.

'You will come back?' she cried, clinging to Marina. 'You really are going to marry Uncle James, aren't you?'

Marina hugged the child to her. 'Wild horses won't keep me away from you, sweetie. Or your Uncle James.' And she glanced up at him through swimming eyes, before hugging the weeping little girl some more. 'I'll be back before you know it. But I have to go home for a little while to sell my mother's house and collect some more clothes. I hardly have a thing to wear, you know, and that's a dreadful thing in a lady's book. Much worse than having no hair.'

'Nothing's worse than having no hair!' Rebecca cried plaintively.

Marina pulled back and wiped the child's tears from her cheeks while she struggled to stop her own. 'You're so right,' she agreed. 'But in no time you'll have more hair than you'll know what to do with. And you'll be so well! Your Uncle James and I are going to take you home as soon as I get back, and you'll never have to come here again. Except perhaps for the odd check-up. But then I'll be with you, and I won't leave you alone for a second.'

Rebecca drew back to raise her big green eyes in the most heart-wrenching way. 'Promise?'

'Cross my heart.' Which she did with her finger.

The child threw her arms around her again. 'Oh, Marina, I love you!'

'And I love you too, darling. Now, let's get you undressed and into bed before I get into trouble from the sister. You wouldn't want to get me into trouble, would you?'

'You're so good with her,' James complimented her on the drive back to the apartment. They were sitting together on the back seat of the Bentley. James's arm was around Marina's shoulder and her cheek was resting on his chest.

Marina bit her bottom lip. She was feeling awfully fragile. What on earth would they do if Rebecca was not better when she came back? What if the transplant hadn't worked? What if the cancer returned with a vengeance?

Suddenly it all became too much for her. 'Oh, James!' she cried, and buried her face in his chest, the tears which had threatened in the hospital room flowing down her cheeks.

'Yes, I know,' he said quietly, holding her close and letting her cry. 'But someone quite wonderful recently told me that we must have faith. We must believe. And I do believe, Marina. I believe it was no rare coincidence that your name popped out of that register. Your being sent over here to save Rebecca's life was a type of destiny. It had been written. I'm not sure how or why, but it was. Rebecca is going to get well. She is going to live as surely as we're going to get married and live happily ever after. I know it.'

'Oh!' Marina gasped, and sat upright, wiping her tears away. 'Oh, I just realised! I didn't before. I was worried you might not be happy about it, but now I see how silly I'm being, because it's me you love, not someone's daughter. Yet being that person's daughter is why this happened, why I was a near perfect match. Oh, James, darling, you're so right. It *was* written. It *was*!'

He cupped her face and stared deep into her eyes. 'Marina, I don't have the foggiest clue what you're talking about.'

'No, of course you don't. And I wouldn't have— yesterday. But today, in the boatshed, you said something and I realised.'

'Realised what?'

'That my being a near perfect match with Rebecca was not a coincidence. You see, I'm not a stranger who just happened to have the right blood and tissue type. I'm a relative!'

'A *relative*?'

'Yes, my mother's maiden name, James, was Bingham! Rebecca's maternal grandmother—Joy Bingham—was my mother's twin sister. My mother was Jocelyn Bingham.'

'Good God!' he exclaimed. But then he laughed. 'Marina, that's just so incredible!'

'Yes, I know,' she said. 'Just think! You ended up with one of the notorious Bingham girls.'

He grinned. 'You mean one of those bad girls who married men for their money?'

'My mother didn't!' Marina defended. 'She married for love!'

'So she did. Just like her darling daughter. You do love me, don't you?' he asked as he gathered her to him once more.

'I love you so much,' she murmured, 'that it's positively indecent.'

'Mmm. Do you think you might sneak upstairs into my room tonight when Henry's asleep? I mean, if you're going to be away for three weeks, I'll need a little something to remember you by.'

'Are you sure I can trust you out of my sight for that long?'

'Are you sure I can trust you back there in sunny Australia with that Shane fellow?'

'Yes.'

'Give me your word.'

'You have it.'

'And you have mine.'

She sighed her contentment and snuggled into him.

'One thing you must learn about us Marsden men,' James told her as he stroked her hair, 'is that we have been notorious rakes down the years, but once we fall in love and marry it's for good. Nothing—and I mean nothing—will ever stop me loving you, Marina. That's the nature of *this* beast.'

'I like the sound of that.'

'We're just turning down the mews.'

Marina sat upright with a swift resurgence of nerves. 'Oh, dear God. Henry!'

James chuckled. 'Don't be afraid of Henry. He's a lamb in wolf's clothing.'

'I…I just want him to approve of me.'

'He *does* approve of you.'

'No, he doesn't. I think he thinks I'm a hussy.'

James grinned. 'You *are* a hussy.'

'And *you're* a rake!'

'See how well matched we are?'

'Oh, you…you…'

He kissed her, then helped her out of the car. William was pretending not to have seen or heard a thing, but Marina thought she saw the corners of his mouth twitching. And his eyes were definitely laughing at them. She found some comfort in that, for at least William approved of her.

Henry was waiting in the foyer to give them a welcome so un-Henry-like that Marina was rendered speechless. He smiled rather smugly at James, then flummoxed Marina by actually hugging her.

'I've just heard the wonderful news,' he announced, drawing back to stand with ramrod straightness once more. 'First from Lady Tiffany, then from Mildred. I can't tell you how delighted I am, My Lord, that everything has worked out so well.'

'Tiffany contacted you?' James asked.

'Yes, My Lord. To reassure me, I think, that she too was happy about the situation. I must admit I *was* relieved. I have always greatly admired Lady Tiffany, but there is something about Miss Marina, here, which is so hard to resist.'

'*Very* hard, Henry.'

'I could see that last week, My Lord. I did feel for you, and the dilemma you were in. I hope you will forgive me,' he went on, looking decidedly sheepish, 'but I…er…engaged in a little subterfuge myself in order to give you a push in the right direction.'

'Really? What subterfuge, Henry?' James asked, frowning.

'Yes, what subterfuge, Henry?' Marina echoed, intrigued.

'The Bentley was not really in for service last Friday night,' he admitted.

James sucked in a sharp breath. 'Are you saying your ordering that limousine was deliberate?'

'I thought you and Miss Marina could do with some time alone together. Away from here, and in more…romantic…surroundings.'

'Henry, you have genuinely shocked me!'

Me too, Marina thought.

'I find that hard to believe, My Lord.' Henry was back to his po-faced best. 'Being your valet over the years has broadened my mind considerably in matters dealing with the opposite sex. I merely thought of what *you* might have done a little while back, when your mind was not clouded by feelings of duty.'

'Yes, well, enough of past history, Henry,' James said briskly. 'I think we should move on to the present. Mildred rang too, you said?'

'Indeed, My Lord. She was beside herself with happiness for you and Miss Marina. She's so looking forward to Winterborne Hall being a family home again, with the patter of little feet to shake some dust off the portraits—especially those lining the staircase.' Henry's eyes twinkled in fond memory. 'Remember how you used to slide down the banister, Jamie-boy?'

Marina stared at Henry. Why, James was right! Henry was just an old fraud, with his stiff upper lip and his stuffy old ways. Underneath that starchy façade he was just a big softie, not to mention a romantic.

'My God, don't go telling Marina things like that, Henry!' James exclaimed, though laughingly. 'I'm already having enough trouble maintaining her respect. Now she not only thinks I'm a rake, but a rascal as well!'

'I think Henry's the rascal,' Marina said, and came forward to reach up and give him a kiss. 'But a lovable rascal.'

Henry actually blushed. It was a sight to behold.

'After James and I are married,' she said, 'whenever we stay at Winterborne Hall you're coming with us, Henry. And not to the gatehouse, either. You will have a room near the nursery. Talbot and Mildred are going to need all the help they can get once I start having babies.'

'But I know nothing about babies, Miss Marina.'

'Then you'll have to learn, Henry. Because I might have to have quite a few. Girls run in my family, and at least one boy is the order of the day, is it not? Now, I think we need one of your excellent pots of coffee, Henry.'

'Yes, Miss Marina.'

Marina gave an exasperated sigh. 'And no more of that Miss Marina stuff, either.'

Henry gave her request some thought before saying, 'Yes, I suppose Miss Marina really won't be appropriate, under the circumstances. All right. Would you like something to eat with your coffee, My Lady?'

Marina groaned. But then she shook her head and laughed helplessly. 'I give up. You both win. I'll be a good Roman.'

'Roman?' Henry repeated blankly. 'I'm sorry, My Lady, but I don't understand.'

Now James laughed. 'Don't even try, Henry. Don't even try. Just lead on to the kitchen.

'I must say I like the thought of our having lots of babies,' he whispered, after Henry had moved off. 'Having Rebecca with me has definitely sparked my fathering instincts. And I don't really mind if you don't have a boy.'

'Well, if I don't, then you can only blame yourself. It's actually the man who determines the sex of the child. But, knowing you, I'll have a boy straight away. In fact, it's quite possible that a little heir and Earl might be already on the way. You didn't use any protection in the boatshed, and today is right in the middle of my cycle.'

'Really?' he said eagerly.

'James Marsden!' she chided. 'Were you trying to make me pregnant on purpose?'

'Er...'

'Oh, James! You are worse than a rascal. You're a...a...'

'A man desperately in love,' he finished for her fiercely. 'Who doesn't want the woman he loves having any reason to change her mind.' He stopped and pulled her to him and kissed her soundly.

'I have only one thing to add at this point in time,' he ground out when he let her come up for air.

'What?' she asked breathlessly.

'I hope Henry goes to bed early.'

'You mean unshockable Henry?' Marina asked, smiling. 'The one who sent us off in that boudoir on wheels? The same Henry who saw you through all your wild years?'

'You're right!' James pronounced, and straightened his spine. 'Henry?' he called out gruffly.

'Yes, My Lord?' came the answer from the kitchen.

'Cancel the coffee. Marina and I are going to bed!'

There was only the minutest of hesitations in answering. 'Very good, My Lord.'

# EPILOGUE

MARINA stood next to her husband in the small stone church, built over nine hundred years ago in Norman times, a far cry from St. Paul's Cathedral, where they'd been privileged enough to be married just over nine months previously.

*At least I didn't disgrace myself by having a baby too soon after the wedding,* she thought, smiling. Little Harry hadn't been conceived till after she'd returned from her trip back to Sydney.

It had taken her just on a month to tie things up in Sydney—slightly longer than the three weeks she'd promised James.

Shane hadn't been too broken-hearted when she'd given him his ring back, especially when it had come with the horses and the business name of the riding school. He *had* been shocked for a split second by her announcement she was going to marry the Earl of Winterborne, because he'd imagined James to be an elderly gentleman. When he'd quickly concluded— with smug predictability—that she was marrying for money, Marina had found herself letting him think so. It had soothed Shane's ego somewhat and amused her to death.

In the end Shane had taken out a bank loan on the

strength of his equity in the horses and riding school and purchased the house and property from Marina, which had meant everyone was happy. But the loan and the exchanging of contracts had taken time.

By the time she'd arrived back in London James had been predictably keen to show her his love in more than words, which he had done over the next week with overpowering passion and at odd times. Marina had been breathless at the chances he took. But when the urge overtook James, he could be very forceful. She would never be able to go into his bank building again without blushing madly.

Marina wondered idly whether Harry had been conceived in the lift between the ninth and tenth floors, or on the boardroom table. She rather fancied the latter, which, after all, had been the scene of many a merger. Though none quite so...exciting. Just thinking about it made Marina's heart beat faster.

Little Harry started to cry at that moment, snapping Marina back to the moment at hand. The vicar had started pouring the holy water over his forehead and Harry was not at all impressed.

Henry clucked and cooed the infant back to sweet silence with all the experience of six weeks being Harry's first emergency nanny, and now his godfather.

Marina leant over towards James. 'Henry's got a real knack with Harry, hasn't he?' she whispered.

'You won't be saying that when he starts imbuing him with all those starchy old ideas of his,' he whispered back. 'And when he insists on the boy being sent away to school at the tender age of eight.'

'A lot you know. Henry and I had a little chat the other morning—around two o'clock, it was—and we both decided Harry wasn't going anywhere for a long, long time.'

James sighed. 'Between the two of you, I don't think I'm going to have any say at all in the raising of my own son.'

'You chose his name, didn't you?'

'I chose Henry. And you promptly changed it to Harry.'

'Just to save confusion, old chap,' she said with a public school accent, then grinned up into James's startled face. 'Just being a good Roman.'

'Whatever am I going to do with you, Marina?'

'I'll show you tonight. The doctor's given me the green light.'

She loved the sound of her husband's intake of breath, plus the squeezing of her hand. 'Just in time, too,' he muttered under his breath. 'There are only so many exercises I can do to take my mind off things. Rebecca says I'm beginning to look like Arnold What's-his-name.'

At the mention of Rebecca, Marina's sparkling eyes shifted from Henry and the baby in his arms to the cute little girl standing next to him in the very feminine apple-green dress, her slender hand on the hem of Harry's long white Christening robe. She had grown so pretty, with her once bald head now covered in red-gold curls the exact colour of Marina's. The specialists had given her the all-clear some months back, although they would continue to monitor her for some time to come.

'Look at Rebecca's face,' James whispered when it came to the part where the godparents had to say something. 'She's so proud to be Harry's godmother. It was a lovely idea of yours to ask her, Marina.'

'She's like a *real* little mother to Harry. I've never known a child love another child so much.'

'She told me the other night she wanted you to have at least six babies.'

'Only six? She told me ten!'

'Er...I thought I'd better water the number down a little before you got ideas.'

'Me? Get ideas?'

'Yes, My Lady,' he whispered drily. 'Already you've swept through Winterborne Hall like a whirlwind, with your radical Aussie ways, changing my normally sensible staff into doting, drooling idiots after your making all of them part-time nannies to Harry! Now what's this I hear about you converting the gatehouse into a pre-school?'

'Well, there isn't one for miles and I rather miss teaching, James. I always did like infants better than older children, and I thought this was a way of killing three birds with one stone.'

'*Three* birds?'

'Yes. It will provide a valuable service for our children and others in the village. It will prevent my getting teacher's itch. And I'll be able to do something with that monstrosity. Brighten it up a bit. Maybe I'll paint it pink.'

'Pink!'

'Okay, I'll leave the outside up to you and your sandblasters. But inside there's going to be lots of colours. And I'm going to have a garden and playground out the back. What do you think?'

'I think you're marvellous.'

'I mean about the idea, silly.'

'I think it's marvellous too.'

'So I have your approval?'

'Go for your life.'

Her eyes danced up at him as she smothered a laugh.

'What?' he said. 'What did I say?'

'That was a very Aussie expression. You'd better watch it or you won't even be a Roman any more yourself. Now hush up. Henry's frowning at you, Jamie-boy.'

James opened his mouth to protest, then closed it again to smile wryly at his wife.

Marina was smiling herself. With happiness.

*Thank you, God,* she prayed, despite not having been brought up to be overly religious. But she'd come to have a great respect for the Almighty since he'd answered her other prayers regarding Rebecca.

*Thank you for darling little Harry, who is utterly perfect. Thank you for keeping Aunt Jasmine and Aunt*

*Janet alive till I found them. They are much nicer than I imagined.*

She cast a quick, smiling glance over her shoulder at the two handsome ladies a couple of rows back. They were dripping in diamonds and pearls, and both childless widows in their late fifties, after the elderly titled gentlemen they'd married in their twenties had long passed on. Despite being rich beyond belief, they seemed to be genuinely thrilled at meeting up with their long-lost niece and being drawn into such a happy—and more normal—family environment.

Marina's gaze shifted to the left and she exchanged smiles with Tiffany and her gorgeous Italian. They had been married for just on six months and were divinely happy, especially now that Tiffany was expecting.

Sighing her satisfaction with life in general, Marina turned back to face the front and resume her conversation with the Lord.

*Thank you for Henry's continuing good health. And Mildred's. And especially Rebecca's. But most of all thank you for my darling husband, who truly does love me for the person I am and not for any other reason.*

'Amen,' James said, and Marina's head jerked up to stare at him. Goodness, had he read her mind? Seen into her thoughts? She hoped not. Sometimes her thoughts were not quite fit for a husband's consumption.

'It's over at last,' he explained into her questioning face. 'The christening.'

'Oh.' Her eyes swept over her handsome husband and she thought of all those exercises he'd been doing and how marvellous he was looking.

Fervently she added her last prayer.

*And please, Lord, please let Harry sleep right through the night tonight!*

# VIVA LA VIDA DE AMOR!

## *They speak the language of passion.*

In Harlequin Presents®, you'll find a special
kind of lover—full of Latin charm. Whether
he's relaxing in denims or dressed for dinner,
giving you diamonds or simply sweet dreams,
he's got spirit, style and sex appeal!

*Latin Lovers* is the new miniseries
from Harlequin Presents® for anyone
who enjoys hot romance!

Meet gorgeous Antonio Scarlatti in
## THE BLACKMAILED BRIDEGROOM
by Miranda Lee, Harlequin Presents® #2151
available January 2001

And don't miss sexy Niccolo Dominici in
## THE ITALIAN GROOM
by Jane Porter, Harlequin Presents® #2168
available March 2001!

*Available wherever Harlequin books are sold.*

He's a man of cool sophistication.
He's got pride, power and wealth.
He's a ruthless businessman, an expert lover—
and he's one hundred percent committed
to staying single.

Until now. Because suddenly he's responsible
for a BABY!

# HIS BABY

An exciting miniseries from Harlequin Presents®
**He's sexy, he's successful...**
**and now he's facing up to fatherhood!**

On sale February 2001:
### RAFAEL'S LOVE-CHILD
by Kate Walker, Harlequin Presents® #2160

On sale May 2001:
### MORGAN'S SECRET SON
by Sara Wood, Harlequin Presents® #2180

And look out for more later in the year!

*Available wherever Harlequin books are sold.*

HARLEQUIN®
*Makes any time special* ™

Visit us at www.eHarlequin.com          HPBABY

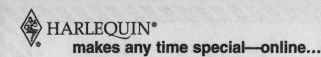

**HARLEQUIN®**

## makes any time special—online...

eHARLEQUIN.com

## shop eHarlequin

♥ Find all the new Harlequin releases at everyday great discounts.

♥ Try before you buy! Read an excerpt from the latest Harlequin novels.

♥ Write an online review and share your thoughts with others.

## reading room

♥ Read our Internet exclusive daily and weekly online serials, or vote in our interactive novel.

♥ Talk to other readers about your favorite novels in our Reading Groups.

♥ Take our Choose-a-Book quiz to find the series that matches you!

## authors' alcove

♥ Find out interesting tidbits and details about your favorite authors' lives, interests and writing habits.

♥ Ever dreamed of being an author? Enter our Writing Round Robin. The Winning Chapter will be published online! Or review our writing guidelines for submitting your novel.

If you enjoyed what you just read,
then we've got an offer you can't resist!

# Take 2 bestselling love stories FREE!

# Plus get a FREE surprise gift!

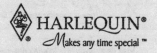

**Lindsay Armstrong...**
**Helen Bianchin...**
**Emma Darcy...**
**Miranda Lee...**

## Some of our bestselling writers are Australians!

Look our for their novels about the Wonder from Down Under—where spirited women win the hearts of Australia's most eligible men.

THE **AUSTRALIANS**

### Coming soon:

## THE MARRIAGE RISK
by Emma Darcy
On sale February 2001, Harlequin Presents® #2157

### And look out for:

## MARRIAGE AT A PRICE
by Miranda Lee
On sale June 2001, Harlequin Presents® #2181

*Available wherever Harlequin books are sold.*

**HARLEQUIN®**
*Makes any time special ™*